FRESHMAN FROST

A PARANORMAL HOLIDAY ROMANCE

NORTH POLE UNIVERSITY
BOOK ONE

MARIE-HÉLÈNE LEBEAULT

BEACHES AND TRAILS
PUBLISHING

CHAPTER ONE
NEW TERM, OLD EXPECTATIONS

FIONA

The sleigh bells still echoed in my ears as the enchanted transport touched down on North Pole University's snow-kissed landing platform. I pressed my mittened hands against the frosted window, watching other students disembark with the easy confidence of those who belonged. My breath fogged the glass as I exhaled slowly, trying to calm the arctic butterflies performing aerial maneuvers in my stomach.

You're a Prancer, I reminded myself, gripping the leather portfolio that contained my acceptance letter. *You belong here.*

All that stood between me and proving I deserved this spot: orientation, a new roommate... and surviving the infamous Frost Trials that had made legends out of students.

But belonging and proving it were two entirely different things.

The sleigh door opened with a crystalline chime, and winter air rushed in, carrying the scents of pine, peppermint, and something indefinably magical that made my reindeer instincts prick with awareness. I gathered my courage along with my luggage—a trunk that levitated obediently behind me, spelled with the finest magic Dad's contacts could provide.

"First time at NPU?" asked the sleigh attendant, a cheerful snow sprite whose silver hair sparkled with actual snowflakes. Her knowing smile suggested she'd seen plenty of nervous freshmen. She glanced at the passenger manifest in her hands, then back at me with obvious recognition.

"That obvious?" I managed a laugh that sounded steadier than I felt.

"Honey, you've got that deer-in-headlights look. No pun intended." She winked, her ice-blue eyes twinkling. "You'll do fine."

I forced a smile and nodded, shouldering my enchanted messenger bag as I stepped onto the platform.

North Pole University spread before me like a winter wonderland brought to life by the most imaginative artist possible. Crystalline spires twisted toward the aurora-painted sky, their surfaces reflecting rainbows that danced across the snow. Buildings carved from what looked like pearl and ice gleamed in the perpetual twilight, connected by covered walkways that sparkled with embedded starlight. In the distance, the famous Frost Tower rose above everything else, its peak disappearing into a swirl of enchanted clouds.

Students moved across the campus in groups, their laughter creating puffs of glittering vapor in the crisp air. I spotted reindeer shifters easily enough—they moved with a particular grace, their eyes bright with inner light. But there were others too: elves with their elegant pointed ears and otherworldly beauty, sprites dancing through the air on gossamer wings, and beings whose species I couldn't immediately identify.

My gaze caught on something that made my chest tighten

with familiar pressure. There, carved into the side of the Crystal Dining Hall in gleaming ice that never melted, was a mural depicting last year's legendary sleigh team. Nine reindeer in perfect formation soared across the frozen tableau, led by one whose antlers seemed to catch and hold starlight even in carved form.

Connor Prancer. My cousin. He'd just had his breakthrough Christmas Eve flight eight months ago, finally proving the Prancer name still meant something. Now we were both at NPU—both first-years, despite his legendary status—both trying to live up to what that name was supposed to represent. His record-breaking flight had earned him fame across campus, but he was still navigating the same academic challenges as any new student.

Even rendered in ice, he seemed to be watching me with those confident Prancer eyes, silently asking: *Are you worthy of the name?*

"Fiona Prancer?"

I jerked my attention away from the mural to find a student approaching with a clipboard that seemed to be writing on itself. She was clearly a snow leopard shifter, her silver-spotted hair catching the light and her pale eyes holding that predatory focus unique to the big cats.

"That's me." I straightened my shoulders, channeling every ounce of confidence I'd inherited from generations of Prancer pride.

"I'm Sera, your student guide. Welcome to NPU." She glanced at her self-updating clipboard, then at the mural behind me. "Ah, admiring Connor's handiwork? That's quite the legacy to live up to. Planning to follow in those hoofprints?"

And there it was. "I'm hoping to make my own path, actually."

Sera's eyebrows rose slightly, but her smile remained diplomatic. "Of course. Well, let's get you settled in Shifter Lodge first, then I'll show you to orientation. Fair warning—Professor Blitzen is giving the welcome address this year, and she's... intense. She was Connor's mentor, actually. I'm sure she'll be watching your progress with interest."

Perfect. More eyes on me, more expectations to either meet or spectacularly fail to reach.

As we walked through the campus, Sera pointed out landmarks with the practiced ease of someone who'd given this tour many times before. The Enchanted Library, where books occasionally flew off shelves to find their intended readers. The Crystal Dining Hall, where hot chocolate flowed from actual chocolate fountains, and the ceiling showed a live view of the aurora borealis. The Sleigh Engineering Workshop, where the sounds of hammering and the glow of magical forges could be seen through frost-covered windows.

"And over there," Sera gestured toward a collection of elegant buildings that seemed to be made entirely of compressed snow and silver, "is Frost Tower. That's where the ice magic students live. Elves, mostly, though we have a few frost giants and the occasional winter witch."

The buildings were beautiful in a way that made my chest tight—not just architecturally, but magically. Even from this distance, I could feel the pull of old power, ancient and precise. The crystal pendant my grandmother had given me—a Prancer family heirloom—grew warm against my throat.

"Do they interact much with the shifters?" I asked, curious despite myself.

"Not really. They tend to keep to themselves. Very formal, very... proper." Sera's tone suggested she found their formality amusing. "Though we do have mixed classes sometimes. Advanced Weather Magic, Seasonal Balance Theory, that sort of thing. And of course, everyone participates in the Frost Trials together."

Shifter Lodge turned out to be everything I'd dreamed of and more. The main building was constructed from living wood, its branches intertwining to form walls and creating small alcoves filled with ever-blooming winter roses. Inside, the common room was warm and inviting, with a massive fireplace that crackled with flames that shifted from gold to green to blue. Comfortable furniture clustered around low tables, and tall windows offered stunning views of the northern lights.

"Your room's on the third floor," Sera said, leading me up a staircase where the banister was carved to look like a frozen stream. "You're sharing with Brynn Foxworth—she's a red fox shifter from Alaska. Super sweet, but fair warning, she's already decorated half the room in what she calls 'arctic chic.'"

My room was indeed half-decorated in white fur throws and crystal accents that caught and reflected light in mesmerizing patterns. A note on the bed written in looping script read: *Welcome, roomie! Gone to find the good hot chocolate. There's mint tea in the kettle if you need caffeine. —B*

I set my luggage down and moved to the window, which offered a perfect view of the main campus courtyard. Students were gathering there now, their colorful winter clothing bright against the snow as they headed toward what I assumed was orientation.

That's when I saw him.

He moved through the crowd like winter itself—silent, graceful, and somehow separate from everyone around him. Tall and lean, with the kind of aristocratic bearing that suggested centuries of good breeding, even though he couldn't be much older than twenty. His hair was the color of moonlight on fresh snow, and even from this distance, I could see the pointed ears that marked him as an elf.

But it wasn't his obvious beauty that made me stare. It was

the way the other students unconsciously moved out of his path, the way conversations seemed to quiet slightly when he passed. There was power there, the kind that didn't need to announce itself because everyone could feel it.

He paused in the courtyard, and for a moment, his head tilted up toward my window. Even three floors up and half a campus away, when his eyes met mine, I felt it like a shock of cold lightning straight through my chest.

Ice-pale blue eyes, ancient and knowing, held mine for exactly three heartbeats. My grandmother's pendant flared with sudden heat against my skin, and for just an instant, I could have sworn I saw frost patterns spreading across my window—patterns that matched the rhythm of my suddenly racing heartbeat.

Then he looked away and continued walking, leaving me gripping the windowsill and wondering why I suddenly felt like I'd forgotten how to breathe properly.

"You okay?" Sera asked from behind me. "You look like you've seen a ghost."

"Who was that?" I managed, one hand unconsciously touching the now-cool pendant at my throat.

Sera followed my gaze to the courtyard, though the mysterious elf had already disappeared into the crowd. "Which one?"

"The elf. Tall, white hair, moves like—"

"Oh." Her voice went carefully neutral. "That would be Elian Frost. Transfer student who just arrived this term, I think, but nobody's quite sure where he transferred from. Very formal, very... reserved. Keeps his distance."

"Frost?" The name sent an odd shiver down my spine that had nothing to do with the temperature.

"Yeah, I know, right? Perfect name for a frost elf. Some of the girls think he might be from one of the old royal families—his manners are certainly formal enough—but he never talks about his background." Sera shrugged. "Honestly, most people find him a bit intimidating. Beautiful, but cold. You know the type."

I didn't, actually. But something about the way he'd looked at me, the way my family pendant had reacted to his presence, suggested that maybe I was about to learn.

"Come on," Sera said, checking her watch. "Orientation starts in ten minutes, and trust me, you don't want to be late for Professor Blitzen's welcome speech. She once made a student run laps around the entire campus for showing up thirty seconds late."

I gathered my things, but as we left the room, I couldn't resist one more glance out the window. The courtyard was empty now except for a few scattered snowflakes that danced in the wind like tiny dancers.

But I could still feel those ice-blue eyes on me, like frost tracing the surface of something long frozen in my heart—something that had just begun to thaw.

CHAPTER TWO
A CHILL INTRODUCTION

ELIAN

The ancient tapestries lining the halls of Frost Tower whispered secrets in languages older than the university itself, but none of them held answers to the question that had been haunting me since I'd arrived at North Pole University three weeks ago: *Why here? Why now?*

I moved through the corridors with the measured pace that had been drilled into me since childhood, my footsteps silent on floors carved from a single sheet of enchanted ice that never melted. Other students—mostly elves like myself, with a scattering of frost giants and winter witches—nodded respectfully as I passed. They maintained the proper distance, as they had been taught. As was expected.

As was safe.

My chambers occupied the highest floor of the tower, a privilege afforded to students of... certain bloodlines. The rooms were exactly what one might expect for someone of my station: elegant, austere, and utterly impersonal. Furniture crafted from crystallized breath of winter itself, walls that showed glimpses of the aurora borealis on command, windows that could display any view of the North Pole I desired.

I chose to keep them clear. Reality was complicated enough without adding illusions.

The letter that had brought me here sat on my desk, its royal blue seal broken, but the magic within still pulsing faintly. I didn't need to read it again—every word was burned into my memory—but I found myself reaching for it anyway.

Prince Elian,

Your presence is required at North Pole University for reasons that will become clear in time. Do not question this directive. Do not contact the court. Complete your studies and await further instruction.

Your devoted servant, Chancellor Arcturus

P.S. The Frost Court's continued... stability may depend upon your cooperation.

The threat was subtle but unmistakable. My father might be the Frost King, but there were powers within the court that had grown restless in recent years. Powers that saw my tendency toward independence as a liability rather than a strength.

So here I was, exiled in all but name to a university filled with hopeful young supernaturals who dreamed of careers in holiday magic, seasonal weather management, and gift distribution logistics. Playing at being a normal student while trying to determine what game the court was truly playing.

A soft chime indicated someone at my door. I waved my hand, and the ice parted like curtains to reveal Professor Glacier, the ancient frost giant who served as Frost Tower's advisor.

"Your Highness," she said, inclining her massive head just enough to show respect without bowing. Technically, I outranked her, but Professor Glacier was older than most mountains and had earned the right to certain informalities.

"Professor," I replied, gesturing for her to enter. "To what do I owe the pleasure?"

Her smile revealed teeth like crystalline daggers. "Orientation begins in twenty minutes. I thought you might benefit from a reminder that punctuality is considered a virtue here, even among those accustomed to having time bend to their will."

A gentle rebuke, elegantly delivered. I had, perhaps, been somewhat cavalier about university schedules since my arrival. Time moved differently in the Frost Court—seasons shifted at our whim, moments could be stretched or compressed as needed. The rigid adherence to mortal concepts of scheduling felt... limiting.

"Of course," I said, rising from my chair. "I wouldn't want to disappoint Professor Blitzen."

"No," Professor Glacier agreed, her tone dry as arctic wind. "You most certainly would not. She has a particular interest in promising students from notable families." Her pale eyes fixed on me with knowing intensity. "I trust you remember our conversation about maintaining appropriate... discretion regarding your background?"

How could I forget? The professor had made it clear that my presence at NPU was meant to be unremarkable. A transfer student from an obscure frost elf academy, nothing more. No mention of courts or crowns or the political machinations that had landed me here.

"I remember," I assured her.

"Excellent. Oh, and Elian?" She paused at the door. "Try to interact with your fellow students occasionally. Isolation breeds suspicion, and suspicion breeds questions we'd prefer not to answer."

After she left, I moved to my window and looked out over the campus courtyard. Students were beginning to gather, their excited chatter rising like steam in the cold air. Reindeer shifters bounded through the snow with natural grace, their eyes bright with anticipation. Sprites darted between groups, their gossamer wings leaving trails of glittering ice crystals. Even from this distance, I could feel their hopes and dreams pressing against my consciousness like eager flames.

It had been so long since I'd been around anyone who felt... young. Hopeful. Unguarded.

In the Frost Court, every emotion was calculated, every expression weighed for political advantage. Here, these students wore their hearts as openly as their winter coats, and something deep in my chest ached at the sight.

Movement in one of the Shifter Lodge windows caught my attention. A girl with auburn hair that caught the light like burnished copper was standing at the glass, and even from this distance, I could sense the restless energy radiating from her. A reindeer shifter, clearly, though there was something different about her magical signature. Something that made my own power stir in response.

Our eyes met across the courtyard, and the world tilted.

I felt it like a physical blow—not painful, but shocking in its intensity. Her magic called to mine with a resonance I'd never experienced, like two notes struck in perfect harmony. For just a moment, the careful walls I'd built around my power wavered, and frost spread across the courtyard stones in patterns that matched the sudden racing of my pulse.

The last time my magic had responded like this was during my coronation ceremony, when the ancient crown of winter had recognized my claim to the throne. But this was different—not the cold acknowledgment of birthright, but something warm and alive and utterly unexpected.

She was beautiful, but that wasn't what left me struggling to breathe. Beauty was common enough among the magical species.

No, it was the way she looked at me—direct, unafraid, curious rather than calculating. As if she saw not a prince to be handled carefully, but simply... me.

I forced myself to look away and continue walking, but I could still feel her gaze on me like warm sunlight against ice. My magic continued to respond to her presence even as I moved away, reaching toward her across the distance like a plant seeking light.

Dangerous, I thought. *She's dangerous.*

Not to my person—I could defend myself against any physical threat. But to the careful control I'd spent years perfecting, to the emotional distance that kept me safe from court intrigue and political manipulation. She threatened all of that simply by existing, simply by looking at me like I mattered beyond my title and bloodline.

I needed to stay away from her.

The Crystal Auditorium was already filling when I arrived, students claiming seats in groups that reflected the university's social hierarchies. I chose a seat near the side wall, close enough to show respect for the proceedings but far enough from the main groups to avoid unwanted social interaction.

Professor Blitzen took the stage with the kind of entrance that reminded everyone exactly why she was considered one of the most formidable educators in the supernatural world. Lightning —actual lightning—crackled between her fingers as she moved, and her silver hair seemed to move in a wind that touched nothing else.

"Welcome," she said, her voice carrying easily through the auditorium without magical amplification, "to North Pole University, the premier institution for supernatural education and the training ground for tomorrow's leaders in holiday magic."

Her pale eyes swept the crowd, lingering for just a moment on faces that clearly meant something to her. When her gaze found mine, I felt the weight of assessment behind it. She knew who I was—of course, she did. The question was what she intended to do with that knowledge.

"You are here," she continued, "because you have demonstrated exceptional ability, unwavering dedication, or remarkable potential. Some of you come from families with long traditions of service to the seasonal courts. Others are the first of your lines to pursue magical education."

Her attention shifted toward the shifter section, and I found myself following her gaze until I spotted the copper-haired girl from the window. She sat with perfect posture, hands folded in her lap, but I could see the tension in her shoulders. The weight of expectation settled around her like a visible cloak.

"Excellence," Professor Blitzen said, her voice sharp as winter wind, "is not inherited. It is earned. Every day, through every choice, in every challenge you face. The name you carry into these halls means nothing if you cannot prove yourself worthy of it."

The girl's hands tightened almost imperceptibly. *Ah.* So she carried a name that meant something here. Interesting.

"This year's freshman class will face the Frost Trials in three months' time," the professor continued, and I felt the energy in the room shift to keen attention. "These trials have tested students for over two centuries, measuring not just magical ability, but character, resilience, and the capacity to work as part of a team."

She gestured, and the air above the stage shimmered into an image of students working together to navigate what looked like a magical blizzard. Ice and snow swirled around them as they supported each other, their combined magic creating pathways through the storm.

"You will be assigned partners," she said, and several students exchanged nervous glances. "These partnerships are not suggestions—they are requirements. Your success will depend entirely on your ability to trust, communicate, and synchronize your magical abilities with someone who may be completely unlike yourself."

The image shifted to show a reindeer shifter and a frost elf working together, their different magical signatures blending into something stronger than either could achieve alone. My power stirred again, responding to possibilities I didn't want to consider.

"Partner assignments will be posted tomorrow morning," Professor Blitzen announced. "I suggest you spend this evening getting to know your fellow students. The trials begin in October, and failure means expulsion from the program."

The weight of that statement settled over the room like a thick blanket. Expulsion wasn't just academic failure—it meant disgrace, the end of magical career prospects, return to families who had invested everything in their children's success.

For someone like me, it would mean a return to the court and whatever fate Chancellor Arcturus had planned.

The rest of the orientation passed in a blur of administrative details and faculty introductions. I maintained appropriate attention while my mind raced through possibilities and implications. The Frost Trials would require a partner, someone I would need to trust with not just my academic success, but potentially my freedom.

Someone who might discover exactly who and what I really was.

As students began filing out of the auditorium, I caught another glimpse of copper hair in the crowd. The girl was surrounded by other shifters now, their conversation animated and warm in a way that tugged at something lonely in my chest.

I had spent my entire life surrounded by people who knew my every move carried political implications. Here was someone who might look at me and see only Elian, not Prince Elian, not a chess piece in court games, not a symbol of power or alliance.

Dangerous, I reminded myself again. But as I watched her laugh at something one of her new friends said, I couldn't quite bring myself to care.

Tomorrow, the partner assignments would be posted. Tonight, I would return to my crystalline chambers and plan for every possible scenario.

I told myself it didn't matter. That I could handle anyone's fate assigned to me. But I already knew the truth—there was only one name I dreaded and hoped to see in equal measure.

CHAPTER THREE
CLASHING PATHS

FIONA

The morning air bit sharp and clean as I hurried across campus toward the Central Plaza, where the partner assignments were supposed to be posted. My boots crunched through fresh snow that sparkled like crushed diamonds in the early light, each step sending small puffs of powder into the air.

I'd barely slept, my mind churning through every possible scenario. What if I was paired with someone who couldn't keep up? What if they expected me to carry the team on the strength of the Prancer name alone? What if they were one of those students who whispered about Connor behind my back, comparing every move I made to his legendary performances?

What if you're paired with him?

The thought hit me like a snowball to the face, stopping me mid-stride. The mysterious Elian Frost, with his ice-pale eyes, and the way my pendant had reacted to his presence. I shook my head firmly. The odds were astronomical. There had to be at least sixty students in the freshman class, and plenty of other ice magic users who would make more logical partners for a frost elf.

"Fiona! Wait up!"

I turned to see Brynn jogging toward me, her red hair flying like a banner behind her. My roommate had boundless energy even at seven in the morning, which should have been illegal. Her fox shifter heritage showed in the graceful way she moved across the uneven ground, never once losing her footing despite the slippery conditions.

"Please tell me you didn't actually get up at five to practice shifting forms again," she panted as she caught up to me.

"Six," I corrected, falling into step beside her. "And it's called preparation, not obsession."

"Honey, when you're practicing the same aerial maneuver seventeen times before breakfast, it's an obsession." She bumped my shoulder affectionately, her breath creating small clouds in the frigid air. "You know you're already one of the strongest shifters in our year, right? Professor Hoof practically glowed when she watched your form yesterday."

Professor Hoof's approval meant a lot—she was notoriously difficult to impress, having trained three Olympic-level reindeer shifters in her career. But her praise didn't quiet the voice in my head that whispered *not good enough, not like Connor.*

As we approached the Central Plaza, I could see we weren't the only ones who'd arrived early. Small clusters of students had already gathered around the massive crystal bulletin board, their voices carrying across the snow-muffled courtyard in excited whispers and nervous laughter.

"There's Marcus," Brynn pointed toward a tall figure with pale blond hair who was pacing near the fountain. "He looks about as nervous as you do."

Marcus Winterberry was a snow owl shifter from Alaska who

seemed as focused on academics as athletics. We'd met briefly during orientation activities, and I'd noticed he looked as nervous about the academic challenges ahead as I felt.

"And there's trouble," I muttered, spotting a familiar group near the board.

Lysander Winters stood with three other ice magic students, their pale heads bent together in what looked like serious conversation. Even from this distance, I could see the way other students gave them a wide berth—not out of fear, exactly, but out of recognition that they operated on a different level than the rest of us.

"Ice magic royalty," Brynn said, following my gaze. "I heard Lysander's family has connections to multiple seasonal courts— Frost, Summer, Spring, and Autumn. That kind of political influence across the court system opens doors the rest of us will never see."

"Lucky him," I replied, though I couldn't keep the bitterness entirely out of my voice. Court connections meant advantages I'd never have, no matter how hard I worked.

"Hey." Brynn stopped walking and grabbed my arm, forcing me to face her. "You're spiraling. I can see it in your eyes."

"I'm not spiraling. I'm being realistic about—"

"You're scared." Her fox-sharp hearing had caught the tremor in my voice that I'd tried to hide. "Fiona, you're here because you earned it. Whatever partner you get, they're going to be lucky to work with you."

Before I could argue, a commotion near the bulletin board caught our attention. Students were pressing forward, voices rising in excitement as the crystal surface began to shimmer and glow.

"It's starting," someone called out.

"Everyone, back up! Give it room to display properly!"

"I can't see anything from here!"

The crowd surged forward despite the calls for order, and I felt my heart begin to race. This was it. In the next few minutes, I'd know who would share my fate for the remainder of the semester.

Professor Blitzen materialized at the edge of the plaza with a sharp crack of displaced air, her silver hair crackling with electrical energy. Lightning danced between her fingers as she surveyed the crowd with the expression of someone who'd dealt with anxious students for far too many years.

"Form orderly lines," she commanded, her voice carrying easily across the plaza despite not being magically amplified. "Everyone will have the opportunity to view their assignments. Pushing and shoving will result in detention, which I guarantee is less pleasant than whatever partnership anxiety you're currently experiencing."

The crowd reluctantly sorted itself into more manageable groups, though the excited chatter continued unabated. I found myself swept along in the general movement toward the board, Brynn's hand warm and steadying on my elbow.

"Breathe," she murmured. "Whatever happens, we'll figure it out."

The crystal board was a work of art in itself—a massive sheet of what looked like compressed starlight that responded to magical commands. As we watched, elegant script began to appear across its surface, names pairing themselves in neat columns that would determine the next several months of our academic lives.

FROST TRIALS PARTNERSHIPS - YEAR ONE

The heading appeared first, followed by a subtitle that made my stomach clench: *Assignments are final and non-negotiable. Appeal processes are limited to cases of documented magical incompatibility.*

Non-negotiable. So whatever fate awaited me on that board, I'd have to live with it.

Names began appearing in alphabetical order, and I found myself holding my breath as each partnership was revealed. Some pairings made obvious sense—magical types that traditionally worked well together, students whose abilities would complement each other naturally. Others seemed designed to challenge preconceptions, pairing earth magic with air magic, or shifters with elemental users.

"Brynn Foxworth and Marcus Winterberry," Brynn read aloud as her name appeared about halfway down the board. "Oh, excellent! He's that nice snow owl shifter from Advanced Flight Theory."

I barely heard her response. My eyes were scanning frantically for my own name, my heart hammering against my ribs. Please let it be someone reasonable. Someone competent. Someone who wouldn't look at me and see only the shadow of my famous cousin.

And then I found it, about three-quarters of the way down the board:

Fiona Prancer & Elian Frost

The world tilted sideways.

"Oh," Brynn breathed beside me. "Oh my."

I stared at the names, willing them to rearrange themselves into something that made sense. But there they were, linked together in Professor Blitzen's precise handwriting: my name and his, bound together for the next three months of trials that would either launch our magical careers or destroy them entirely.

The conversations around us seemed to fade into background noise as the implications hit me. Elian Frost—the mysterious transfer student with his ice-pale eyes and aristocratic bearing. The one who'd made my pendant react like it was recognizing something ancient and powerful. The one who moved through crowds like winter itself, silent and separate and somehow fundamentally *other*.

"This has to be a mistake," I said faintly, though even as the words left my mouth, I knew better. Every pairing was carefully calculated based on magical compatibility, personality assessments, and academic potential.

"Honey, Professor Blitzen doesn't make mistakes. She makes strategic decisions." Brynn's voice carried a note of sympathy that made my situation sound even more daunting. "Maybe it won't be so bad? I mean, he's gorgeous, and—"

"And completely wrong for this." I found my voice again, louder than I'd intended. Several students turned to look at us, their expressions ranging from curious to pitying. "Ice magic and reindeer shifting? We're fundamentally incompatible. Our magical signatures will clash constantly."

But even as I said it, I remembered the way my pendant had warmed in his presence, the frost patterns that had appeared on my window. Maybe incompatible wasn't exactly the right word. Maybe the problem wasn't that our magic would clash—maybe it was that it would work too well together, in ways I didn't understand.

And that terrified me more than failure ever could.

Because what if working with Elian didn't just challenge my magical abilities? What if it changed them entirely? What if it changed *me* entirely? I'd spent my whole life trying to fit into the Prancer mold, trying to become the reindeer shifter my family expected. What if this partnership demanded I become someone completely different—someone I didn't even recognize?

The thought made my chest tight with a fear that had nothing to do with academic performance and everything to do with losing myself in the process of becoming whatever this magic wanted me to be.

"Well, look on the bright side," Brynn said, checking her own assignment again with obvious relief. "At least you won't be bored."

Bored. That was definitely not going to be a problem.

Around us, other students were having similar realizations about their partnerships. I caught snippets of conversation—excitement, disappointment, confusion, the occasional outright dismay. Near the front of the crowd, I heard someone arguing with Professor Blitzen about their assignment, their voice rising in what sounded like panic.

"Professor, surely there's been some kind of error. I specifically requested—"

"Mr. Ashworth," Professor Blitzen interrupted coolly, "your requests were noted and subsequently ignored. Partnership assignments are based on optimal magical development potential, not personal preference."

"But the compatibility indices—"

"Are calculated using factors far more complex than your first-year understanding of magical theory can encompass." Her tone suggested the conversation was over. "I suggest you focus your energy on making the partnership successful rather than arguing with the decision."

Optimal magical development potential. The phrase echoed in my mind as I stared at my name linked with Elian's. What had Professor Blitzen seen in our magical signatures that made her think pairing us was optimal for anything other than mutual frustration?

"You should probably find him," Brynn said gently. "Get this first conversation over with before the anxiety kills you."

She was right, of course. Standing here staring at the board wasn't going to change anything, and the longer I put off dealing with this partnership, the worse it was going to get.

My eyes were already scanning the crowd, looking for a familiar head of moonlight-pale hair. I needed to find Elian and figure out how we were going to make this work. Or if we were going to make this work.

That's when I felt it—a presence behind me that made the air suddenly cooler and charged with power. The same sensation I'd experienced when I'd first seen him in the courtyard, like winter itself had taken human form.

"Fiona Prancer."

The voice behind me was crisp, cultured, and unmistakably cold. I turned slowly, and there he was—tall, elegant, and looking about as thrilled with our partnership as I felt.

Up close, he was even more striking than he'd been from my window. His features were sharp and aristocratic, carved from ice and starlight with the kind of precision that suggested centuries of selective breeding. His pale hair was perfectly arranged despite the wind that had been tousling everyone else's, and his winter-blue eyes held depths that seemed far older than his apparent age.

But it was the way he *moved* that really caught my attention—with the unconscious confidence of someone who'd never doubted his place in the world, never questioned whether he belonged somewhere. It was the opposite of everything I felt about my own presence at NPU.

"Elian Frost," I replied, grateful that my voice came out steady despite the butterflies performing aerial acrobatics in my stomach. "I suppose we need to talk."

"Indeed." He glanced around at the crowd of chattering students, many of whom were openly staring at us now. The mysterious transfer student and the Prancer heir—we probably made quite a picture. "Perhaps somewhere more private would be appropriate."

Private. The word sent an odd shiver down my spine that had nothing to do with the temperature. There was something in the way he said it—not suggestive exactly, but weighted with implications I couldn't quite parse.

"The Enchanted Library has study rooms," I suggested, my mind already racing ahead to our conversation. What was I supposed to say to him? How did you negotiate a partnership with someone who clearly operated on a completely different level than you did?

He nodded once, a sharp, economical movement that somehow managed to convey both agreement and dismissal. "Lead the way."

As we began walking across campus, I was acutely aware of the space between us—close enough for conversation, far enough to maintain the invisible barrier he seemed to carry everywhere. Other students moved out of our path, whether because of the ice crystals that seemed to form in Elian's wake or the restless energy radiating from me, I couldn't tell.

The silence stretched between us, neither comfortable nor entirely hostile. More like the quiet before a storm, when the air itself holds its breath waiting to see what will happen next.

"You seem displeased," Elian said finally, his tone carefully neutral.

"I'm... concerned about the practical implications," I replied, choosing my words carefully. "Our magical systems are fundamentally different."

"An understatement." He paused in his walking, turning to look at me directly. "Tell me, Miss Prancer, what do you know about ice magic?"

The formal address stung, but I pushed past it. "It requires precision, control, and emotional distance. Everything reindeer shifting isn't."

Something that might have been approval flickered in his expression. "And what does that suggest to you about this partnership?"

"That Professor Blitzen either sees something we don't, or she's conducting some kind of experiment in magical incompatibility."

"Or," he said quietly, and for just a moment, his perfect composure seemed to slip, revealing something almost... uncertain beneath, "she's trying to teach us both something we can't learn on our own."

His voice carried a weight that suggested he was speaking from experience—someone who'd spent a long time learning things alone, perhaps longer than he should have.

The possibility hadn't occurred to me, but as we resumed walking toward the library, I found myself considering it. What could I possibly learn from someone whose entire magical philosophy seemed opposed to everything I believed about power and emotion and connection?

What could he learn from me?

And more unsettling still—what if the learning required becoming someone I'd never been before? What if the Fiona who emerged from this partnership bore no resemblance to the one who'd entered it?

Maybe that's the point, a treacherous voice whispered in my mind. *Maybe the person you've been trying so hard to be isn't who you're supposed to become.*

By the time we reached the Enchanted Library, I was no closer to answers, but I was beginning to suspect that the next few months were going to challenge everything I thought I knew about magic—and myself.

The question was whether either of us would survive the experience with our magical abilities—and our sanity—intact.

CHAPTER FOUR
TRIAL PAIRING

ELIAN

The library had always been one of my preferred locations—neutral ground, with enough ambient magical energy to mask the more unusual aspects of my own power signature. If we were going to have a conversation that might reveal more than I intended, better to have it somewhere the walls themselves were accustomed to keeping secrets.

The private study room she led us to was smaller than I'd expected, lined with books that hummed softly with contained knowledge. As the door closed behind us, I felt the familiar weight of isolation lift slightly. Here, at least, we could speak without the constant awareness of watching eyes and listening ears.

But the intimacy of the space also made me acutely aware of her presence in ways I hadn't anticipated. The way she moved with unconscious grace, the subtle scent of winter pine that clung to her hair, the warm golden energy that seemed to emanate from her very being.

She's dangerous to everything you've worked to protect.

"I assume you're as concerned about this arrangement as I am," I said, moving to the window to put some distance between us. The snow-covered campus spread below, peaceful and deceptively simple.

"Concerned?" She settled into one of the chairs, studying me with those direct eyes that seemed to see more than they should. "I'm worried about the practical implications, yes. Our magical systems are fundamentally different."

"An understatement." I turned to face her, allowing myself to really look at her for the first time. There was strength in her posture, intelligence in her gaze, and something else—a restless energy that spoke of power carefully contained. "Ice magic requires precision, control, and patience. Reindeer magic is..." I paused, searching for diplomatic phrasing.

"Instinctive? Emotional? Inferior?" The words came out sharp, her temper flaring in response to what she'd clearly interpreted as condescension.

"I was going to say unpredictable," I said quietly, and something in my tone made her look at me more carefully. "Though I suppose from my perspective, that amounts to the same thing."

From my perspective. The words carried more weight than I'd intended, revealing the fundamental truth I'd been trying to hide —that my perspective had been shaped by a lifetime of fearing exactly the kind of unpredictability she represented.

"And what perspective is that?" she asked, her voice carrying a challenge I hadn't expected. "Ice magic superiority?"

The question hit closer to the mark than she could have known. Not superiority—survival. The cold, careful control that had kept me alive for twenty years in a world where emotional magic was viewed as a liability at best and a fatal weakness at worst.

"The perspective of someone who's been taught that unpredictability is dangerous," I admitted, the words slipping out before I could stop them. "That emotional magic is a liability. That trusting your instincts will get you killed."

As I spoke, I felt something shift in the magical atmosphere of the room. The books on the shelves seemed to lean in closer, as if sensing that secrets were being shared. And from my hands, without conscious direction, silver light began to spiral in patterns that matched the rhythm of my suddenly racing pulse.

Frost spread across the window in delicate spirals, and I realized with growing alarm that my careful control was slipping in response to her presence. The magical compatibility that Professor Blitzen had somehow detected was real, pulling at defenses I'd spent years perfecting.

"That sounds like a lonely way to live," Fiona said softly, and the unexpected gentleness in her voice made something tight in my chest begin to loosen.

Lonely. Yes, that was exactly what it was. Twenty years of isolation, of careful distance, of never allowing anyone close enough to see past the facades I'd constructed.

"Loneliness is safer than the alternative," I replied, though even as I said it, I could feel the truth of that belief beginning to waver. "At least, that's what I've always been told."

"Always been told." She leaned forward slightly, and I could see her processing the distinction between belief and indoctrination. "But what do you think?"

The question caught me off guard. When was the last time anyone had asked what I thought, rather than what I'd been taught or what was expected of me?

"I think," I said slowly, "that partnership magic requires exactly the kind of trust I've been trained to avoid. And I think that makes me a poor choice for someone whose success depends on magical collaboration."

"Or," she said, rising from her chair to stand closer to the window where frost patterns were still spreading from my unconscious magical leakage, "it makes you someone who understands the risks involved and can help ensure we approach this partnership carefully."

The silver light emanating from my hands grew brighter, reaching toward her warm golden energy like metal drawn to a magnet. Where our magical signatures touched, the air itself seemed to sing with harmonic resonance that made my teeth ache.

This is what Professor Blitzen saw, I realized. *This compatibility defies everything I know about magical theory.*

"Can I ask you something?" Fiona said, her own magic beginning to respond to our proximity.

"You can ask. I may not answer."

"Yesterday, in the courtyard, when we looked at each other..." She touched something at her throat—a pendant I now noticed was glowing faintly with warm light. "Did you feel that? The recognition, or whatever it was?"

Recognition. Yes, that was exactly what it had been. The sense that my magic was responding to something it had been searching for without my knowledge.

"Yes," I admitted. "I felt it."

"What do you think it meant?"

I was quiet for a long moment, watching the way our magical energies wove together in the air between us despite neither of us consciously directing them. Everything I'd been taught suggested this kind of uncontrolled magical resonance was exactly what I should fear and avoid.

But looking at the beauty of the patterns we were unconsciously creating, feeling the way my magic seemed to settle into harmony rather than chaos when it touched hers...

"I think," I said carefully, "that Professor Blitzen knows things about magical compatibility that aren't covered in first-year textbooks."

"That's not exactly an answer."

"No," I agreed. "It's not."

But it was as close to honesty as I dared come. Because the real answer—that her magic felt like coming home to a place I'd never known I was searching for—was too dangerous to voice aloud.

"So what do we do?" she asked, settling back into her chair as our magical display slowly faded to manageable levels. "Pretend that whatever happened yesterday was meaningless and hope we can muddle through the next few months without failing spectacularly?"

"Or," I said, the words coming from some part of me that had apparently decided caution was less important than possibility, "we acknowledge that there's something between us that neither of us understands, and we try to figure out what it means."

The suggestion sent visible tremors through her magical aura, and I realized she was as affected by our connection as I was. The difference was that she seemed willing to explore it, whereas my every instinct was screaming warnings about exposure and vulnerability.

"That sounds dangerous," she said, echoing my own thoughts.

"Everything worthwhile is dangerous." The words came from somewhere deep in my memory—Master Wynne's voice, full of gentle encouragement for a seven-year-old prince who was afraid to trust his own magical instincts. "The question is whether we're brave enough to find out what we might become together."

What we might become together. The phrase hung in the air between us like a promise and a threat in equal measure.

"You're not what I expected," she said finally.

"What did you expect?"

"Someone colder. More arrogant. Someone who would look at me and see a convenient way to pass the trials without having to do much work himself."

The assessment stung because it was probably accurate for most people in my position. But it also revealed something about her own fears—that she expected to be used, dismissed, seen as less than worthy of real partnership.

"The Prancer name carries weight here. Connor's success opens doors. Surely that occurred to you when you saw our names paired together."

I didn't know how to respond to that.

"You don't know who Connor is," she said suddenly, studying my expression. "Do you?"

Connor. The name meant nothing to me, though I could see from her reaction that it should.

"Should I?" I asked.

"He's my cousin. The golden boy who restored our family's honor and became the youngest lead reindeer in three centuries." Her voice carried a mixture of pride and something that sounded like resignation. "Most people who know the Prancer name know Connor's story."

Most people. But I wasn't most people. I was someone who'd spent twenty years in hiding, deliberately isolated from the kind of social networks that would make family legends common knowledge.

"I don't know who Connor is," I said simply. "I don't know what doors the Prancer name might open, or what advantages it might provide. All I know is that when I looked at you in that courtyard, something in my magic... woke up. Something that's been dormant for longer than I care to admit."

The honesty of the admission surprised me as much as it seemed to surprise her. But sitting here in this quiet room, watching the way her magic responded to mine with such perfect harmony, I found I was tired of the careful calculations that had governed every interaction for the past two decades.

"I felt it too," she said quietly, and as she spoke the words aloud, the magical resonance between us intensified again. "Like my magic was recognizing something it had been looking for."

Exactly. That was exactly what it had felt like.

"Then perhaps," I said, "we should stop fighting it and start exploring what it might teach us."

Exploring. The word carried implications that made my pulse quicken. Not just magical exploration, but personal. Emotional. The kind of deep connection I'd been trained to fear and avoid.

"I have conditions," she said, straightening in her chair with sudden determination.

"Conditions?"

"No more calling me Miss Prancer like we're strangers. If we're going to do this, we're going to do it as equals." Her eyes held mine steadily. "And no more pretending that whatever brought us together was pure chance. Something made Professor Blitzen pair us specifically, and I want to know what."

"Fair enough," I said, finding myself genuinely impressed by her directness. "And my conditions?"

"You have conditions too?"

"Trust works both ways, Fiona." Using her name felt strange and right in equal measure. "I need to know that you won't run the moment things get complicated. That you won't decide this partnership is too difficult and find a way to transfer to someone safer."

The request revealed more about my fears than I'd intended—not just about academic failure, but about abandonment. About being left alone again just when I'd started to hope for something different.

"I don't run," she said firmly. "Prancers see things through to the end, even when—especially when—those things seem impossible."

"Good," I replied, and for the first time since receiving my assignment to NPU, I felt something that might have been hope. "Because I have a feeling impossible is going to be our specialty."

As we prepared to leave the study room, I felt a fundamental shift in the dynamic between us. We were no longer reluctant partners thrown together by circumstance. We were collaborators, choosing to trust each other with something neither of us fully understood.

The fear was still there—of exposure, of discovery, of the political consequences that would follow if certain parties learned how thoroughly my careful defenses were crumbling. But underneath it was something I hadn't felt in twenty years: anticipation.

The question was whether I had the courage to see where this impossible partnership might lead.

Looking at Fiona, seeing the determination and curiosity that shone in her eyes, I thought I might.

CHAPTER FIVE
TRAINING BEGINS

FIONA

I arrived at the training grounds to find Elian already there, standing motionless in the center of the practice area like a statue carved from winter itself. Frost spread in perfect geometric patterns around his feet, and his breath formed precise clouds in the frigid air.

He was meditating, I realized. Or doing whatever the magical equivalent was for frost elves.

I approached quietly, not wanting to disturb him, but his eyes opened before I'd taken three steps.

"You're early," he observed, straightening with that fluid grace that made everything look effortless.

"So are you. Do you ever sleep?"

Something that might have been amusement flickered across his features. "Sleep is... optional when one has trained in proper meditation techniques."

"Great," I muttered. "I'm partnered with an ice-powered over-achiever. Fantastic."

The corner of his mouth definitely twitched that time. "I'll make note of your need for adequate rest. Professor Hoof left instructions for today's exercises. She is observing from the equipment station, making notes on her ever-present clipboard. We're to work on defensive constructs."

He gestured to a series of targets that had appeared overnight —enchanted projectiles that would fire ice shards, bursts of wind, and what looked suspiciously like miniature lightning bolts. The idea, apparently, was to create barriers that could withstand magical attacks while maintaining structural integrity.

"Any thoughts on approach?" I asked, pleased that he was actually asking for my input instead of just telling me what to do.

"Your magic provides flexibility. Mine provides strength." He studied the targets with clinical assessment. "In theory, a barrier that combines both should be nearly impervious."

In theory. "And in practice?"

"In practice, we'll need to maintain the connection for extended periods while under attack." His pale eyes met mine, and I felt an echo of yesterday's electric sensation. "It will require... trust."

The word hung between us like a challenge. Trust. The thing that had been conspicuously absent from all our interactions so far.

"I can handle it if you can," I said, lifting my chin.

He nodded once, sharp and decisive. "Then let's begin."

This time, when I reached for my magic, I was prepared for the intensity of our connection. The golden warmth flowed from my hands more easily, seeking out the pathways Elian's ice provided. But instead of the gentle weaving from yesterday, this required something deeper—a sustained link that left me feeling exposed and raw.

The barrier we created was a thing of beauty, translucent as glass but strong as steel, with veins of golden light running through crystalline walls. When the first projectile hit it, the impact sent shockwaves through our shared magic that I felt in my bones.

"Steady," Elian murmured, his voice strained with concentration. "Don't pull back."

Easier said than done. Every hit made me want to retreat, to protect myself from the vulnerability of being so completely connected to someone else. But I gritted my teeth and held on, pouring more energy into our construct as the attacks intensified.

By the time Professor Hoof called an end to the exercise, sweat was dripping down my spine despite the freezing temperature. Elian looked equally drained, his usual perfect composure slightly frayed around the edges.

"Excellent work," the professor announced, making notes on her ever-present clipboard. "Your barrier held for the full twenty minutes under sustained assault. Most partnerships manage maybe five on their first attempt."

Most partnerships. Right. Because we were apparently not most partnerships.

"Tomorrow we'll work on offensive constructs," she continued. "I want to see how well you can project combined attacks."

After she left, Elian and I stood in the silence of the training grounds, both of us carefully not looking at each other. The magical connection had been severed, but I could still feel the echo of it, like phantom limbs that ached for completion.

"That was..." I began, then trailed off, not sure how to finish.

"Intense," he supplied quietly.

"Yeah." I rubbed my arms, trying to dispel the lingering sensation of his magic intertwined with mine. "Is it always like that? The connection, I mean."

He was quiet for so long, I thought he wasn't going to answer. Then: "No. It's not."

The admission sent a flutter through my chest that I tried to ignore. "Oh."

"Fiona." The way he said my name made me look at him. Really look at him. The aristocratic mask had slipped again, revealing something uncertain underneath. "What we're doing... the magic we're creating together... it's not normal."

"I kind of figured that out."

"I mean, it's not just unusual. It's..." He ran a hand through his silver hair, disturbing its perfect arrangement. "In my experience, magical partnerships are functional. Practical. They don't feel like..."

"Like what?"

"Like coming home," he said quietly, and my heart did something complicated in my chest.

Coming home. Yes. That was exactly what it felt like.

"Is that a problem?" I asked, though I was pretty sure I already knew the answer.

"It could be." He glanced around the empty training grounds, then stepped closer, lowering his voice. "Professor Glacier mentioned there would be observers monitoring promising partnerships. They're not just university faculty."

A chill ran down my spine that had nothing to do with the temperature. "Who were they?"

"Court representatives. Probably sent to monitor my progress and ensure I'm not... exceeding expectations."

Exceeding expectations. "And creating magical barriers that last four times longer than normal would qualify as exceeding expectations?"

"Among other things, yes."

I stared at him, trying to process the implications. "So we're supposed to fail? Or at least be mediocre?"

"I'm supposed to be unremarkable." His jaw tightened. "Invisible. A minor frost elf with adequate abilities completing his education quietly."

"But you're not a minor frost elf." It wasn't a question.

"No. I'm not." He looked away, his profile sharp against the pale sky. "And if certain people discover just how not minor I am..."

He didn't finish the sentence, but he didn't need to. The threat was clear enough.

"Then we'll be careful," I said, surprised by my own certainty. "We'll find a way to train without drawing attention."

"Fiona—"

"No." I stepped closer, close enough that I could see the flecks of silver in his ice-blue eyes. "Whatever political mess you're running from, we'll figure it out. But I'm not giving up this partnership."

"You don't understand what happens when frost magic binds too tightly to another soul." His voice was barely above a whisper, but the words hit me with the force of a shout. "The consequences aren't just political. They're... permanent."

The way he said *permanent* sent another shiver down me, but not entirely from fear. "Then explain it to me. Trust works both ways, Elian. If you want me to help you stay under the radar, you need to tell me why."

For a moment, I thought he might actually do it. His lips parted as if he was going to speak, and something vulnerable flashed across his features. Then he stepped back, that invisible wall slamming into place again.

"I should go," he said, his voice once again carefully controlled. "Same time tomorrow."

He was three steps away before he stopped and turned back.

"For what it's worth," he said quietly, "I don't want to give up this partnership either."

Then he was gone, leaving me standing alone with my magic still humming restlessly under my skin and the growing certainty that I was falling for someone whose secrets could destroy us both.

But as I walked back toward Shifter Lodge, one thought kept circling through my mind: he'd called it *coming home.*

And if our magic felt like that to both of us, maybe it was worth the risk.

Even if the price of discovery was higher than either of us could afford to pay.

That evening, I found myself in the Enchanted Library, researching everything I could find about frost elf nobility and the politics of the seasonal courts. If Elian wouldn't tell me what we were up against, I'd figure it out myself.

Hours later, surrounded by ancient texts and scrolls that whispered secrets in languages I could barely understand, I finally found something that made my blood run cold.

The Lost Prince of the Frost Court, one leather-bound volume proclaimed, *vanished during the Night of Broken Ice twenty years past. Some say he was killed. Others whisper he was hidden, his very existence a threat to the new order...*

I stared at the words until they blurred, pieces of a puzzle clicking into place with terrifying clarity. A missing prince. A hidden heir. An exile masquerading as a transfer student.

And frost magic that bound too tightly to another soul.

Because the Prancer family didn't back down from a challenge.

And something told me that Elian Frost—whatever his real

name might be—was the biggest challenge and the greatest reward I'd ever face.

CHAPTER SIX
THE EXTRAORDINARY
WORLD

ELIAN

The fourth day of training dawned with an ominous stillness that made my skin prickle with unease. As I made my way to the training grounds, the very air seemed charged with expectation, as if the world itself was holding its breath for something momentous to occur.

The letter from Chancellor Arcturus still sat on my desk, its broken seal a constant reminder of the sword hanging over my head. *Complete your studies without drawing attention,* it had warned. *Avoid magical displays that might reveal your true capabilities.*

I'd managed to follow those instructions for exactly three days.

Yesterday's training session with Fiona had been a revelation and a catastrophe in equal measure. The barrier we'd created together had been flawless—too flawless. The kind of seamless magical integration that should have been impossible for students of our supposed experience level.

And I'd felt eyes watching us. Calculating. Evaluating.

They're coming, I thought as I approached the training area. *The only question is how long I have before they arrive.*

Fiona was already waiting, her auburn hair catching the pale morning light like burnished copper. She looked focused but troubled, her magical signature humming with the kind of restless energy that suggested she'd slept as poorly as I had.

"You're distracted," I observed as we began our warm-up exercises. Her golden magic was flickering inconsistently, responding to emotional undercurrents rather than conscious direction.

"Sorry," she muttered, shaking out her hands and trying to center herself. "I didn't sleep well."

Neither had I, but for reasons I couldn't share. The dreams had come again—memories of the Frost Court, of the night everything had changed, of Master Wynne's final words echoing through twenty years of careful hiding.

Find your partner, he had whispered as the guards dragged him away. *Find the one who makes your magic sing with joy instead of duty.*

Looking at Fiona now, feeling the way our magical signatures resonated even when we weren't actively collaborating, I wondered if Master Wynne had somehow known this day would come.

"Let's try the layered barrier technique," Fiona suggested, but I could sense her heart wasn't fully in the exercise.

As we began to weave our magic together, I felt the familiar harmony that had become as natural as breathing. Golden warmth met crystalline precision, creating something that was both beautiful and impossibly stable.

Too much like the royal collaborative magic that hadn't been seen in three generations.

"Fiona, what—" I started to say, then stopped mid-sentence

as my enhanced senses picked up familiar magical signatures approaching across the training grounds.

My blood turned to ice.

Professor Blitzen was walking toward us, but she wasn't alone. Flanking her were two figures in formal frost elf robes, their magical auras carrying the unmistakable authority of court officials.

Lord Arcturus. Lord Kieran.

They'd found me.

After twenty years of careful hiding, of maintaining perfect anonymity, of following every protocol designed to keep me invisible—they'd found me because I'd been unable to resist the pull of collaborative magic with someone whose power called to mine like a song.

"Prancer, Frost," Professor Blitzen called as they drew near, her voice carefully neutral but her magical signature tense with concern. "A word, if you please."

Play the role, I told myself, slipping into the mask of polite deference I'd perfected over years of hiding. *Give them nothing they can use.*

"Of course, Professor," I replied, my voice perfectly controlled despite the chaos in my chest.

But even as I spoke, I could feel our magical construct wavering as my concentration fractured. The beautiful barrier we'd created began to destabilize, its golden and silver patterns fragmenting into chaotic spirals.

The two court officials studied us with the kind of clinical attention that made my magical defenses want to slam into place. Lord Arcturus—tall, reed-thin, with silver hair and eyes like chips of winter sky—regarded me with the expression of someone who'd been expecting this moment for years.

Lord Kieran, broader and younger but carrying himself with

unmistakable arrogance, focused his attention on our failing magical construct with obvious interest.

"Lord Arcturus," Professor Blitzen said formally, gesturing to the taller official. "Lord Kieran. May I present Fiona Prancer and Elian Frost."

Elian Frost. Even hearing my assumed name spoken in the presence of court officials made something twist in my stomach. How long before they demanded to know my real identity? How long before they connected the dots between the hidden prince and the mysterious transfer student who could channel Deep Magic?

"Miss Prancer," Lord Arcturus said with a slight bow that managed to be both respectful and dismissive. His pale eyes lingered on her for only a moment before shifting to me with laser focus. "We've heard interesting reports about your... partnership."

"All good, I hope," Fiona replied, and I felt a surge of admiration for the steadiness in her voice despite the obvious tension in her magical signature.

"Indeed." Lord Arcturus's attention was entirely on me now, and I could feel him cataloging every detail—my posture, my magical control, the way power seemed to flow naturally from my hands despite my attempts to suppress it. "Mr. Frost. You've been making quite an impression."

The words carried weight beyond their surface meaning. This wasn't a casual compliment—it was an acknowledgment that they knew exactly who I was and what I was capable of.

"I hope my academic performance has been satisfactory," I said carefully, maintaining the pretense that this was about schoolwork rather than bloodlines and political succession.

"Oh, more than satisfactory. Remarkable, one might say." Lord Kieran stepped forward, his gaze calculating as he studied the residual magical patterns still lingering in the air around us. "Tell me, how long have you two been training together?"

The question seemed innocent enough, but I could hear the trap beneath it. How long had it taken for the dormant royal magic to manifest? How quickly had I lost control of abilities I was supposed to keep hidden?

"Four days," Fiona answered when I remained silent, and I felt grateful for her intervention even as I dreaded what would come next.

"Four days," Lord Kieran repeated thoughtfully, as if that timeline held special significance. "And already creating magical constructs that senior partnerships struggle to achieve. Fascinating."

The way he said *fascinating* made it sound like a death sentence.

"The students have been working very hard," Professor Blitzen interjected smoothly, her protective instincts clearly activated despite her own curiosity about what we'd become. "Natural talent combined with dedication often produces extraordinary results."

"Extraordinary," Lord Arcturus mused, and I felt his power pressing against the edges of my consciousness, testing my defenses. "Yes, that's precisely the word I would use."

His attention fixed on me with uncomfortable intensity. "Perhaps you could demonstrate this extraordinary partnership for us? A simple defensive construct should suffice."

It wasn't a request. It was a command wrapped in polite phrasing, and we all knew it.

I glanced at Fiona, seeing my own dread reflected in her carefully controlled expression. We'd barely been able to maintain basic magical harmony when I was distracted by political concerns. Trying to perform under direct scrutiny from court officials who clearly suspected my true identity was courting disaster.

But refusing would be worse than failure. It would be confirmation that I had something to hide.

"Of course," I said, stepping into position and drawing on every lesson in royal composure I'd ever received. My posture was perfect despite the terror coursing through my veins.

Fiona moved to face me, and for a moment our eyes met. In her gaze, I saw determination mixed with confusion, trust layered over fear. She didn't understand what was happening, but she was willing to face it beside me.

Trust me, I tried to convey without words.

She nodded slightly, and I felt her reach for her magic with deliberate focus.

When our powers met, something extraordinary happened. Instead of the chaotic overflow I'd been dreading, our magic flowed together with perfect harmony. Golden warmth and crystalline precision merged into something that was both stronger and more beautiful than either of us could achieve alone.

The barrier we created wasn't just functional—it was art. Delicate frost patterns spiraled through walls of crystallized gold, creating something so breathtaking that even Lord Arcturus drew in a sharp breath.

But as the construct solidified, I realized with growing horror that we'd made a terrible mistake. This wasn't an adequate magical display of promising students. This was the unmistakable signature of royal Deep Magic—the kind of collaborative power that hadn't been seen since my father's death.

"Interesting," Lord Kieran said quietly, and the satisfaction in his voice made my blood run cold.

But it was Lord Arcturus who delivered the killing blow.

"Tell me, young Frost," he said conversationally, never taking his eyes off our barrier, "when did you first discover you could channel the Deep Magic?"

The world tilted on its axis.

My perfect construct shattered like breaking crystal, the sound echoing across the training grounds as every carefully maintained pretense crumbled around us.

Twenty years of hiding. Twenty years of following protocols, maintaining anonymity, suppressing the very abilities that marked me as my father's son.

All undone by the simple act of finding someone whose magic called to mine with a harmony too perfect to ignore.

"I don't know what you mean," I said, though my voice lacked conviction even to my own ears.

"Don't you?" Lord Arcturus smiled, and it was sharp as a blade. "Because this construct bears all the hallmarks of royal ice magic. The kind that hasn't been seen since..." He paused dramatically. "Well. Since the Night of Broken Ice."

The Night of Broken Ice. The night my father had died. The night I'd been spirited away to begin a life of exile and hiding.

The night that had defined every choice I'd made for the past two decades.

"Fascinating indeed," Lord Kieran murmured, his attention shifting between our shattered magical display and my undoubtedly pale face. "Professor Blitzen, I think we'll need to have a more private conversation with these students."

"Of course," she replied, though I could hear the reluctance in her voice. Professor Blitzen had always been protective of her students, but even she couldn't stand against direct court intervention. "My office in an hour?"

"Perfect." Lord Arcturus turned his cold smile on Fiona, and I felt my protective instincts flare despite the hopelessness of our situation. "Miss Prancer, I do hope you understand the... delicate nature of what you've witnessed here today."

The threat was unmistakable, even wrapped in diplomatic language. They were warning her to stay silent about my abilities, about the royal magic I'd just displayed, about everything that could connect Elian Frost to Prince Elian Frostborn.

"I understand that my training partner is exceptionally talented," Fiona replied evenly, and I felt a surge of fierce admiration for her courage. "Beyond that, I'm not sure what you're implying."

Something that might have been approval flickered in Lord Arcturus's expression, but it was quickly replaced by calculating interest.

"How refreshingly naive," he said. "I'm sure that will change soon enough."

As the officials walked away with Professor Blitzen, I stood frozen on the training grounds, the weight of discovery crushing down on me like an avalanche.

"So," Fiona said quietly, moving to stand beside me. "Deep Magic."

I looked at her—really looked at her. This person who'd managed to do what twenty years of court agents and magical investigators had failed to accomplish: force me to reveal exactly who and what I was.

But instead of fear or calculation in her eyes, I saw determination. Loyalty. The kind of fierce protective instinct that had nothing to do with politics and everything to do with partnership.

"Fiona," I began, then stopped. What could I possibly say? How could I explain that falling in love with her—because that's what this was, I realized with startling clarity—might have doomed us both?

"One hour," she said firmly, cutting through my spiral of self-recrimination. "That's how long we have to figure out our story before they start asking questions we can't answer."

Our story. Not my story, not my problems, not my royal complications that she'd been dragged into through no fault of her own.

Our story.

"Together?" I asked, echoing the question that had started this impossible partnership.

"Always," she replied without hesitation.

And despite everything—the political disaster, the exposure of abilities I'd spent a lifetime hiding, the certainty that powerful forces were aligning against us—I felt something that might have been hope beginning to kindle in my chest.

Because I wasn't facing an impossible situation alone.

Everything worthwhile was dangerous, Master Wynne had taught me.

And Fiona Prancer was definitely worthwhile.

CHAPTER SEVEN
MENTORS & MISTRUST

FIONA

Professor Blitzen's office was a study in controlled chaos. Shelves lined every wall, crammed with books that occasionally rearranged themselves, snow globes that showed real weather patterns from around the world, and what looked like a collection of crystallized lightning bolts. Her desk was carved from a single piece of black ice that never melted, and the chairs facing it were decidedly less comfortable than they appeared.

Elian and I sat in those chairs now, waiting. The air between us still hummed with residual energy from our training session—the memory of our magic weaving together in impossible harmony, creating something neither of us could have achieved alone. Even now, sitting carefully apart, I could feel the echo of that connection like a second heartbeat.

Lord Arcturus and Lord Kieran flanked Professor Blitzen's desk like sentries, their expressions unreadable. The professor herself sat behind her intimidating workspace, her silver hair crackling with barely contained electrical energy that made the air taste of copper and storms.

The silence stretched until I thought I might scream from the tension. Every few seconds, I caught glimpses of silver light dancing around Elian's fingers—so faint I might have imagined it, but proof that our earlier magical display had left him as affected as I was.

"Well," Professor Blitzen said finally, her voice cutting through the oppressive quiet like a blade. "This is quite the situation we find ourselves in."

"Indeed," Lord Arcturus agreed, his pale eyes fixed on Elian with laser intensity. "Though I must say, Prince Elian, your performance has been... illuminating."

Prince Elian. Hearing his true title spoken aloud made everything feel terrifyingly real. The stakes weren't just academic anymore—they were political, dynastical, potentially deadly.

Beside me, Elian sat perfectly still, every inch the royal heir he'd been born to be. But I could see the tension in his hands, the way his jaw tightened almost imperceptibly. "Lord Arcturus. Lord Kieran. I assume you have questions."

"Oh, we have many questions," Lord Kieran said, stepping forward with predatory grace. "But let's start with how this partnership has managed to unlock power levels that threaten the stability of inter-court relations."

The question hung in the air like a weapon. I felt my heart hammering against my ribs, remembering the golden and silver threads that had woven between us in the library, the way the very air had seemed to sing when our power merged.

"I haven't manifested anything," Elian replied smoothly, his voice carrying the practiced diplomacy of centuries of royal breeding. "Miss Prancer and I have simply discovered an unusual compatibility in our magical signatures."

Lord Arcturus laughed, the sound sharp as breaking glass. The crystalline artifacts around the office resonated with the harsh note, creating an eerie harmony that made my teeth ache. "Please. Do you take us for fools? What we witnessed today was royal ice magic of the highest order. Magic that's been dormant in your bloodline for generations."

As if responding to his words, frost began to spread across the office windows in delicate, branching patterns. Not random ice formation—these were sigils, ancient symbols that seemed to pulse with their own inner light. I recognized some of them from the oldest magical texts, the ones written before the courts had solidified their current power structures.

"Magic that certain parties were quite certain would never manifest," Lord Kieran added meaningfully, his gaze shifting between the frost patterns and Elian's carefully controlled expression.

I felt Elian tense beside me, though his face never changed. Through our growing bond, I could sense the undercurrent of old anger, fear carefully buried beneath layers of royal training. "And yet here we are."

"Here we are indeed." Lord Arcturus turned his attention to me, and I fought not to shrink under his icy gaze. When he looked at me, the air around my chair grew noticeably warmer—my magic responding defensively to the perceived threat. "Tell me, Miss Prancer, what exactly do you know about your partner's background?"

The question I'd been dreading. I could feel Elian's tension ratcheting higher, though he gave no outward sign of it. Golden light began to spiral faintly around my hands—barely visible, but enough to make Lord Kieran's eyes narrow with interest.

"I know he's a transfer student from an advanced ice magic academy," I said carefully, meeting Lord Arcturus's gaze steadily.

"I know he's incredibly skilled and that our magic works well together. Beyond that, I don't see how his background is relevant to our academic partnership."

The golden light around my hands brightened slightly, and I realized it was responding to my conviction. Not just magical energy, but something deeper—the truth of what I'd said, the honesty of my feelings for Elian regardless of his hidden identity.

"Interesting," Lord Kieran murmured, but something was calculating in his expression as he watched the interplay of light and frost around us.

Professor Blitzen cleared her throat, drawing all attention back to her. Lightning danced between her fingers as she leaned forward, her expression serious. "Gentlemen, while I appreciate the gravity of this situation, these are still my students. I'll not have them intimidated in my office."

"Of course not," Lord Arcturus said smoothly, though his tone suggested he found her protection amusing. "We're simply trying to understand the scope of what we're dealing with. The magic these two created together today was... unprecedented."

As he spoke, the frost patterns on the windows began to shift and change, forming new configurations that seemed to tell a story. I saw images of ancient partnerships, of ice and flame working together to create wonders that defied natural law. The golden light around my hands responded, reaching toward the frost patterns as if drawn by an invisible force.

"Unprecedented, how?" I asked, though I wasn't sure I wanted to know the answer.

Lord Kieran exchanged a look with Lord Arcturus before responding. The moment their eyes met, the magical atmosphere in the room intensified—books on the shelves began to glow softly, their leather bindings warming as if touched by sunlight.

"Royal ice magic has certain properties, Miss Prancer," Lord

Kieran said, his voice carrying new weight. "It doesn't simply create—it transforms. It takes the raw potential of another magical signature and elevates it beyond its natural limits."

The books around us pulsed brighter, as if responding to his words. I could hear whispers emanating from their pages—not words exactly, but something deeper. Knowledge trying to break free from ancient bindings, secrets demanding to be heard.

"What he's saying," Professor Blitzen added gently, though her crackling hair suggested her own magic was responding to the growing power in the room, "is that your magic was amplified far beyond what should have been possible for a first-year student. The barrier you created today could have withstood attacks that would challenge graduate-level partnerships."

The truth of it hit me like a physical blow. I thought about our training session, the way creating that defensive construct had felt effortless despite its complexity. Not just teamwork—transformation. My magic hadn't just worked with Elian's; it had become something entirely new in the process.

I stared at her, trying to process the implications while golden and silver energy continued to dance around us in increasingly complex patterns. "So our compatibility isn't just unusual. It's impossible."

"Under normal circumstances, yes." Lord Arcturus leaned back against the wall, his posture deceptively casual even as frost continued to spread from his position. "But royal ice magic operates under different rules. It seeks out magical signatures that can complement and enhance its own power. In the old days, such partnerships were considered sacred bonds."

Sacred bonds. The words sent a shiver down my spine that had nothing to do with the temperature. Around us, the office had become a light show of responding magical energies—books glowing, frost patterns shifting, lightning crackling, and through it all, the golden and silver threads that connected Elian and me growing stronger and more visible.

"However," Lord Kieran continued, and the warmth in his voice carried a note of warning that made my magic recoil instinctively, "such partnerships were also extremely rare and closely monitored by the court. For obvious reasons."

"What reasons?" Elian asked, though his tone suggested he already knew the answer. The frost patterns on the windows had formed a complex mandala now, beautiful and somehow ominous.

"Because when royal ice magic bonds completely with a compatible signature, the resulting power can reshape the very foundations of magical law." Lord Arcturus's smile was razor-sharp, reflecting the light dancing around us in fractured rainbows. "In the wrong hands, such power could topple governments. Destroy the careful balance that has maintained peace between the courts for centuries."

The office fell silent except for the soft humming of Professor Blitzen's magical artifacts and the almost musical resonance of our combined energies. I could feel my heart hammering against my ribs as the full scope of what we'd stumbled into became clear.

The golden light around my hands pulsed in rhythm with my heartbeat, and I watched as Elian's silver energy synchronized to match it. We weren't just academically partnered anymore—we were magically bonded in ways that apparently threatened the stability of the entire magical world.

"So what happens now?" I asked, surprised by how steady my voice sounded despite the magical storm swirling around us.

"Now," Lord Kieran said, and his pale eyes reflected the dancing lights like mirrors, "we discuss your options."

"Options?" Elian's voice carried the first hint of emotion I'd heard from him since we'd sat down. Around us, the temperature dropped noticeably, and the frost patterns began to pulse with urgent light.

"The court has been watching you for years, Elian," Lord Arcturus explained, and with his words, new images formed in the frost on the windows—a young child being spirited away in the night, safe houses, a life lived in shadows. "Waiting to see if you would manifest your heritage. Until today, we were content to let you complete your education in obscurity. But this changes things."

The images in the frost shifted to show destruction—towers falling, magical storms, partnerships that had ended in catastrophe. A warning, or a threat.

"This meaning our partnership," I said flatly, watching as golden light began to chase through the frost patterns, warming them without melting them.

"This meaning the awakening of power that could threaten the stability of the realm," Lord Kieran corrected. His own magic was visible now—dark blue energy that seemed to absorb light rather than reflect it. "Power that cannot be allowed to develop unchecked."

Professor Blitzen's hair had begun to spark more aggressively, creating a crown of electrical energy around her head. "And what exactly are you suggesting?"

The magical energy in the room was reaching a crescendo—books flying from their shelves to circle overhead, frost covering every surface, lightning crackling between Professor Blitzen's fingers, and through it all, our golden and silver bond growing so bright it cast shadows on the walls.

"Separation," Lord Arcturus said simply, and the word fell into the magical chaos like a stone into still water. Everything went quiet—the flying books, the crackling lightning, even our magical connection seemed to falter at the suggestion. "Miss Prancer will be reassigned to a new partner. Prince Elian will return to the court for proper training in the control of royal magic."

"No." The word was out of my mouth before I could stop it, and with it came a flare of golden energy so bright it temporarily blinded everyone in the room. When the light faded, every book in the office was glowing, the frost patterns had become a complex map of magical connections, and the air itself seemed to hum with power.

Both lords turned to look at me with expressions of mild surprise, as if they hadn't expected me to have an opinion on the matter.

"I'm sorry?" Lord Kieran said, but his voice carried new respect along with the surprise.

"No," I repeated, standing up from my chair. The golden energy around me intensified, and I felt Elian's silver power rise to meet it. "You can't just separate us because our magic works too well together. We haven't done anything wrong."

"Haven't you?" Lord Arcturus asked mildly, but I could see him watching our merged energy with calculation rather than fear. "You've awakened power that has been dormant for generations. Power that certain factions within the court would kill to control."

"Then maybe the problem isn't our magic," I shot back, my temper finally overriding my caution. The books circling overhead began to glow brighter, their pages rustling as if agreeing with my words. "Maybe the problem is a political system so fragile that two students working together threatens to bring it down."

The temperature in the room plummeted.

Ice began to form on every surface, but this wasn't random freezing—these were patterns, sigils, a language written in frost that spoke of power and protest and the refusal to be silenced. But it wasn't coming from the lords or Professor Blitzen.

It was coming from Elian.

"Careful, Miss Prancer," he said quietly, though his eyes had gone almost white with suppressed power, and the air around him shimmered with barely contained energy. "Some truths are more dangerous than others."

The ice spread faster, creating a crystalline map across every surface that seemed to tell the story of our partnership—from that first moment of recognition in the courtyard to the impossible harmony we'd achieved in training. Beautiful, terrible, and completely beyond normal magical law.

I could feel Elian's magic calling to mine, seeking the warmth and stability that would complete the circuit between us. The golden light around my hands reached toward his silver energy like metal to a magnet, and for a moment, I could feel what he was feeling—the weight of royal expectation, the fear of losing the first real connection he'd ever made, the desperate hope that somehow we could find a way to stay together.

Don't, I told myself. *This is exactly what they're afraid of.*

But my magic had other ideas. Golden energy began to spiral around my hands, drawn inexorably toward the frost patterns spreading from Elian's position. Where our energies met, the ice became warm to the touch without melting, and new patterns began to form—not destruction, but creation. Art. Beauty. Proof that our partnership could build rather than destroy.

"Fascinating," Lord Arcturus murmured, watching the interaction with clinical interest rather than fear. "Even under emotional stress, the bond seeks to complete itself. And look—it's not creating chaos. It's creating order. Beauty. Harmony."

Around us, the office had become a gallery of magical art. Every surface told the story of our partnership in light and ice, and floating books arranged themselves in perfect geometric patterns overhead. It should have been chaotic, overwhelming. Instead, it felt like the most natural thing in the world.

"That's enough," Professor Blitzen said, but her voice carried wonder rather than command. Lightning still danced around her, but it had taken on golden and silver highlights that matched our energy. "Both of you, look around. See what you've created."

I blinked, focusing on something other than Elian for the first time since we'd entered the office. The room was transformed—not destroyed, but elevated. Every magical object had become part of a grand design that spoke of partnership and possibility rather than chaos and destruction.

"This," Professor Blitzen said quietly, "is why certain parties want to separate you. Not because your power is destructive, but because it's creative. Because it proves that the old ways of magical isolation aren't the only way."

Lord Kieran was staring at the patterns we'd created, his expression unreadable. "This changes things," he said finally.

"How?" Lord Arcturus asked.

"Because this isn't the chaotic magical explosion we were warned about. This is... collaborative art. Unconscious harmony." He looked directly at Elian and me, and for the first time, his pale eyes showed something other than calculation. "This is what the ancient partnerships were supposed to achieve."

As the immediate crisis passed and our magic began to settle into stable patterns around the room, I felt something shift in the political dynamic. We hadn't just defended our partnership—we'd demonstrated its value in terms even the court observers couldn't ignore.

But the effort had cost us. I could taste copper in my mouth, and when I touched my nose, my fingers came away damp with blood. Beside me, Elian swayed slightly, his perfect composure finally cracking as exhaustion hit him. The beautiful patterns we'd created were already beginning to fade, our magic too drained to maintain them.

"So what does this mean?" I asked, my voice rougher than I'd intended.

"It means," Lord Arcturus said slowly, watching the magical displays flicker and dim, "that perhaps separation isn't the only option after all."

Lord Kieran's expression remained troubled, even as he nodded agreement. "However," he added, his voice carrying a warning that made my newly sensitive magical awareness prickle with unease, "not everyone in the court will be as... appreciative of what you've demonstrated here today. Some view any challenge to the established order as an act of war, regardless of how beautiful that challenge might be."

The question was whether the magical world was ready for what we represented, and whether we could survive long enough to prove our worth to those who saw beauty where others saw only a threat.

Looking around the transformed office, at the fading beauty we'd created unconsciously, at the way even ancient political enemies were staring at our work with something approaching awe, I thought maybe it was.

But Lord Kieran's warning echoed in my mind like a promise of storms to come.

CHAPTER EIGHT

THE STUDY HALL INCIDENT

ELIAN

The morning after our confrontation with the court officials, I stood at my tower window watching the campus come alive below. My reflection in the crystal glass looked drawn, pale even by frost elf standards, and I could see the exhaustion that lingered around my eyes like shadows.

The magical strain from yesterday's encounter had left me feeling raw, exposed. Every time I moved too quickly, silver light sparked involuntarily from my fingertips. My magical senses had become hypersensitive—I could detect energy signatures three floors away, hear the whispered conversations of students passing in the courtyard below.

The confrontation with Lord Arcturus and Lord Kieran had shattered more than just our defensive construct. It had destroyed the carefully maintained illusion that I could complete my education in anonymity, that I could somehow avoid the political machinations that had defined every moment of my life since I was seven years old.

They know, I thought, touching the letter from Chancellor Arcturus that still sat on my desk like a coiled serpent. *They've always known. The question is what they plan to do about it.*

A soft knock at my door interrupted my brooding. I waved my hand, and the ice parted to reveal Professor Glacier's massive form.

"Your Highness," she said quietly, stepping into the room with surprising grace for someone her size. "How are you managing?"

The formal address made me wince. Even here, in what should have been the sanctuary of my private chambers, my true identity pressed against the walls like a caged beast demanding release.

"I've been better," I admitted, moving away from the window. "The magical sensitivity is... intense."

"A common side effect of forced manifestation of Deep Magic," she said, her ancient eyes studying me with concern. "Your magical channels have been expanded beyond their normal limits. It will take time to adjust."

Time I might not have.

"Professor," I said carefully, "how long do you think it will be before they demand my return to the court?"

Her expression grew troubled. "That depends entirely on how much of a threat they perceive your partnership to be. If they believe Miss Prancer's influence is making you stronger, more independent..." She trailed off, but the implication was clear.

They'll separate us by any means necessary.

The thought sent ice spiraling across the floor in agitated patterns. Just the idea of being forced away from Fiona, of losing the first genuine connection I'd felt in twenty years, made my careful control fragment dangerously.

"You care for her," Professor Glacier observed, and it wasn't a question.

"I do." The admission came out quieter than I'd intended. "More than is wise, given the circumstances."

"Perhaps wisdom isn't the most important consideration here," she said gently. "Your father believed that some things were worth any risk."

My father. King Boreas, who had died trying to restore collaborative magic to a world that feared it. Who had believed that partnerships like mine and Fiona's could heal the divisions between magical species.

"My father's beliefs got him killed," I said flatly.

"Your father's beliefs were ahead of their time," she corrected. "But perhaps their time has finally come."

Before I could respond, she glanced toward the window where students were beginning to gather for the day's training sessions. "You should go to her," she said. "Miss Prancer will be wondering where you are."

Fiona. Even thinking her name sent warmth through the ice that had been coating my chambers since yesterday. She would be at the training grounds by now, probably worrying about my absence, maybe even thinking I was avoiding her because of the political complications my identity had brought into her life.

Nothing could be further from the truth.

I found her exactly where I'd expected—standing at the edge of the training grounds, her breath forming small clouds in the frigid air. Even from a distance, I could see the tension in her shoulders, the way her magical signature hummed with restless energy.

The moment I approached, I felt our bond snap into focus like a compass finding north. The hypersensitive chaos in my magical channels settled into something manageable, the constant background static fading to a whisper.

She centers me, I realized with a mixture of wonder and terror. *Even when everything else is falling apart, she makes me feel whole.*

"You're early," I observed, though my voice came out rougher than I'd intended.

"So are you," she replied, turning to face me with those direct eyes that seemed to see straight through every defense I'd ever constructed. "Are you feeling it too? The... sensitivity?"

Among other things. "Everything feels amplified," I said, stepping closer. As the distance between us decreased, the magical strain I'd been fighting all morning eased considerably. "Magical signatures I couldn't detect before are practically screaming at me now."

Her expression softened with understanding. "I keep getting these flashes of magical awareness that feel like someone's playing music too loud in my head."

The price of pushing beyond our normal limits, I thought, remembering Professor Glacier's explanation. But looking at Fiona now, seeing the way our magic naturally harmonized even in our current oversensitive state, I found I couldn't regret what we'd awakened between us.

"The price of yesterday's... confrontation," I said aloud. "Our magical channels have been expanded. Professor Glacier says it will take time to adjust."

"Is that good or bad?"

"Both, probably." I glanced around the training grounds, my enhanced senses picking up familiar magical signatures lurking just beyond the visible area. "It means we're more powerful, but also more vulnerable. And more visible to those who know what to look for."

Speaking of which...

"We're being observed," I said quietly, not wanting to alarm her but needing her to understand the scope of what we were facing.

"I can feel them too," she replied, her voice barely above a whisper. "At least three different signatures. They're not trying very hard to hide from enhanced senses."

The fact that she could detect court surveillance with such precision sent both pride and worry spiraling through my chest. Pride because it proved how much her abilities had grown. Worry because it confirmed that yesterday's magical display had changed her as fundamentally as it had changed me.

"Should we leave?" she asked.

"And go where? They'll follow us anyway." I moved closer, close enough that anyone watching would think we were having an intimate conversation rather than discussing the political forces aligning against us. "Besides, running would only confirm that we have something to hide."

The warmth of her proximity settled the last of the magical chaos in my system. Whatever was happening to us, it was easier to bear when we were together.

"Have you given any thought to a strategy for today?" I asked, though my attention was split between our conversation and cataloging every magical signature within a hundred-yard radius.

"I was thinking we could start with basic compatibility exercises," she replied, matching my casual tone while her golden energy spiraled in defensive patterns I could sense but not see. "See how our new... capabilities affect our standard techniques."

Sensible. And careful. "Though I should warn you—everything feels different now. Stronger. More..." I searched for the right word.

"Intimate," she supplied, color rising in her cheeks.

Yes. The connection between us had evolved beyond simple

magical compatibility into something that felt essential, necessary. I sometimes forgot where my emotional state ended and hers began.

"We'll need to be very careful about maintaining control," I said. "Especially with an audience."

As if summoned by my words, Professor Hoof appeared at the edge of the training grounds, her clipboard already scribbling notes. Behind her came additional figures I didn't recognize—more court observers, their formal robes and calculating expressions marking them as officials sent to monitor our every move.

The price of yesterday's revelation.

"More watchers," Fiona muttered.

"The cost of proving we're too powerful to ignore," I replied grimly. "Apparently, word has spread about what happened in Professor Blitzen's office."

Through our bond, I could feel her touching her nose reflexively, remembering the nosebleed that had marked the end of our unconscious magical collaboration.

"Do you think they're here to shut us down?" she asked.

"I think they're here to determine whether we're worth the risk we represent." I found her hand with mine, and immediately felt our magical connection stabilize into something stronger than either of us could maintain alone. "Which means we need to prove that we are."

But as the court observers positioned themselves around the training grounds like pieces on a chessboard, I couldn't shake the feeling that the game being played was far more complex than either Fiona or I understood.

The real question wasn't whether we were strong enough to handle the magical challenges ahead. It was whether we were clever enough to navigate the political minefields that surrounded us without losing ourselves—or each other—in the process.

Looking at Fiona, seeing the determination that blazed in her eyes despite the obvious pressure we were under, I felt something that might have been hope beginning to kindle in my chest.

Whatever they threw at us, we would face it together. And perhaps, for the first time in twenty years, that would be enough.

CHAPTER NINE
FOUND FAMILY

FIONA

Three weeks into training with Elian, I was finally starting to feel like I belonged somewhere.

It wasn't just the partnership—though our magical collaboration had become the most natural thing in the world, our ice and light weaving together like they'd been meant to find each other. It was everything else: late-night study sessions in the Shifter Lodge common room, shared meals where laughter came as easily as breathing, the growing certainty that I'd found my people.

"You're different," Brynn observed as we walked back from Advanced Flight Theory, our breath forming small clouds in the crisp afternoon air. "More... confident, I guess? Like you've stopped trying to prove you deserve to be here."

She was right, though I hadn't really noticed the change happening. Somewhere between learning to trust Elian's magical precision and discovering that Marcus's dry humor perfectly complemented my tendency toward dramatic overthinking, I'd stopped feeling like an impostor wearing someone else's life.

"I think I've just found my rhythm," I said, then paused as a thought struck me. "Actually, no. I think I've found my tribe."

The word felt right. These weren't just classmates or training partners—they were the people who'd seen me at my most frustrated, most vulnerable, most gloriously successful, and had chosen to stick around anyway.

"Speaking of tribe," Marcus said, appearing beside us with the silent efficiency that marked his snow owl shifter heritage, "we're having an impromptu magic theory session in the common room tonight. Professor Hoof assigned that collaborative spellwork project, and I figured we could tackle it together."

Collaborative spellwork. The assignment that had half the first-year class panicking because it required perfect synchronization between multiple magical signatures. Most students were struggling to find compatible partners, but our little group had developed such natural harmony that Professor Hoof had started using us as examples.

"Count me in," I said, feeling that familiar flutter of excitement that came with any chance to push our magical boundaries. "Elian mentioned he might join us if his evening training session with Professor Glacier finishes early."

"How is that going?" Brynn asked, and I heard the genuine concern in her voice that she'd been showing whenever Elian's intensive magical development came up. "The advanced ice magic work, I mean. He always looks completely drained after those sessions."

Through our bond, I could sense Elian in Frost Tower right now—the familiar weight of concentration as he worked through exercises that pushed his abilities to their limits. Professor Glacier had been helping him develop the kind of precise control that would be necessary for whatever political complications awaited him after graduation.

"He's stronger than he sometimes realizes," I said, choosing my words carefully. There were still aspects of Elian's background that weren't mine to share, but I could offer the truth of what I observed. "The training is intense, but it's helping him under-stand capabilities he never knew he had."

What I didn't say was how much our partnership seemed to be accelerating his development. During our training sessions together, Elian's ice magic had begun showing properties that impressed even Professor Hoof—structures so complex and stable they seemed to defy basic magical theory.

"Well, he's lucky to have you as a partner," Marcus said with characteristic directness. "I've seen plenty of magical collabora-tions fail because one person couldn't keep up with the other's development. You two actually seem to be making each other stronger."

Making each other stronger. The phrase resonated through our bond, and I felt Elian's brief pause in concentration as the thought reached him three floors away. Through our connection, I sensed his quiet gratitude for the network of support that had grown around us both.

"That's the goal," I replied, though I was beginning to under-stand that what Elian and I had built together was something rarer than simple magical compatibility.

By the time we reached Shifter Lodge, word had spread about the impromptu study session. I found the common room filling with students whose magical signatures had become as familiar as family—Sera the snow leopard shifter with her fierce intelli-gence, Dylan the arctic fox whose earth magic complemented everyone else's abilities, Aria the winter wolf whose protective instincts had made her the unofficial guardian of our group.

My people, I thought, watching them arrange themselves around the massive fireplace with books and notes and the kind of easy camaraderie that couldn't be forced. *This is what found family looks like.*

"Alright," Marcus said, settling into his favorite armchair with Professor Hoof's assignment sheet. "Collaborative barrier construction. We need to create a defensive structure that incorporates at least four different magical signatures while maintaining stability under magical attack."

"Sounds like a Tuesday to me," Brynn said with a grin, golden fox fire already beginning to dance around her fingers. "Who wants to go first?"

What followed was two hours of the most natural magical collaboration I'd ever experienced. Not the intense, focused work that Elian and I did during formal training, but something easier —magic shared between friends who trusted each other completely.

Sera's earth magic provided the foundation, solid and unshakeable. Marcus's air magic created the structure, invisible currents that shaped and guided the barrier's formation. Brynn's fire magic added flexibility and responsiveness, allowing the construct to adapt to changing conditions. My light magic wove through everything, connecting the different elements into something stronger than any individual contribution.

"This is incredible," Aria breathed as our collaborative barrier took shape above the coffee table—a shimmering dome of light that pulsed with the combined rhythm of our magical signatures. "I can feel all of your abilities, but I can also feel how they're working together."

Together. The word that had become central to everything I valued about NPU, about the partnerships I'd formed, about the person I was becoming.

"That's what collaboration is supposed to feel like," I said, watching the play of different magical energies in our construct.

"Not just adding individual powers together, but creating something entirely new."

Through our bond, I felt Elian's session with Professor Glacier concluding. His magical signature was tired but satisfied, carrying the particular resonance that came from breakthrough understanding. In a few minutes, he'd be joining us, adding his ice magic to our collaborative work.

Family, I thought as conversations flowed around me—Marcus explaining a particularly complex theoretical concept to Dylan, Brynn, and Sera planning weekend explorations of the campus, Aria quietly helping a struggling first-year with basic shifting techniques. *This is what family feels like when you get to choose it yourself.*

When Elian appeared in the common room doorway twenty minutes later, frost patterns still visible on his formal training robes, the entire dynamic shifted to accommodate him. Not because anyone felt intimidated—we'd all grown comfortable with his presence over the past weeks—but because our magical collaboration naturally expanded to include his precise, powerful ice magic.

"How did it go?" I asked as he settled beside me on the couch, close enough that our magical signatures immediately began harmonizing.

"Productive," he replied, though I could feel through our bond that Professor Glacier had pushed him harder than usual. "Professor Glacier says my control has improved dramatically since we started training together."

"Partnership magic," Marcus observed, making notes about our barrier construction for his assignment report. "It's fascinating how working closely with someone can accelerate individual development."

"Speaking of which," Sera said, her snow leopard instincts

picking up on the subtle magical resonance that always surrounded Elian and me when we were together, "would you mind adding your ice magic to our barrier? I'm curious how it would integrate with what we've already built."

I felt Elian's brief hesitation—not reluctance, but the careful evaluation that had become second nature to him. Then, through our bond, I sensed his decision to trust these people who had become important to both of us.

Ice began to spiral from his hands, but this wasn't the formal, controlled magic of his training sessions. This was ice magic shaped by friendship, by the desire to contribute to something beautiful that we were all creating together.

When his power touched our collaborative barrier, the entire construct transformed. What had been shimmering light became crystalline art—ice and fire and earth and air woven together in patterns so intricate they seemed to tell stories. But more than that, I could feel everyone's magical signatures strengthening as they touched Elian's power, as if his ice magic was amplifying our natural abilities rather than overwhelming them.

"That's..." Dylan started, then trailed off, staring at the magnificent structure we'd created together.

"That's royal-level collaborative magic," Aria finished quietly, and I felt the moment when everyone in the room understood that they were witnessing something unprecedented.

But instead of the fear or intimidation I might have expected, I saw wonder in their faces. Recognition that they were part of something special, something that could grow into genuine transformation.

"It's family magic," Brynn said simply, and her words carried the weight of truth that made everyone nod in agreement. "Magic that's shared between people who care about each other."

Through our bond, I felt Elian's surprise at how easily our friends had accepted both his abilities and his place in our group. He'd spent so many years expecting isolation that genuine acceptance still caught him off guard.

This is what you've been missing, I thought, squeezing his hand as our magical construct continued to evolve above us, becoming more beautiful with each passing minute. *This is what it feels like to have people who choose to stand with you.*

As the evening wound down and our collaborative barrier finally dissolved into sparkles of light that danced around the common room, I realized something fundamental had shifted. This wasn't just about individual friendships anymore, or even about my partnership with Elian.

We had become something larger—a network of connections that strengthened everyone involved. A chosen family that had grown around the foundation of trust and shared magical discovery.

"Same time next week?" Marcus asked as people began gathering their books and notes.

"Absolutely," I replied, and felt the unanimous agreement ripple through our group. "Though I have a feeling our next collaboration is going to be even more interesting."

Found family, I thought as Elian and I walked upstairs together, our magical signatures still humming with the harmony we'd created. *This is what it feels like to be home finally.*

And looking back at the common room where golden firelight played over faces that had become precious to me, where laughter still echoed from conversations that ranged from magical theory to weekend plans to the kind of gentle teasing that only happened between people who truly cared about each other, I knew that whatever challenges lay ahead, we would face them together.

Not just Elian and me, but all of us—a family we'd chosen, magic we'd shared, connections that had made us stronger than any of us could be alone.

CHAPTER TEN
ELIAN'S PAST

ELIAN

The dreams always came when I was most content.

Three nights after Lord Kieran's warning about betting pools and enemies, three nights after Fiona had looked at me with such fierce loyalty that it made my chest ache with unfamiliar warmth, the familiar nightmare dragged me back to the world I'd been running from for twenty years.

I stood in the Crystal Throne Room of the Frost Court, but I was seven years old again, small hands pressed against the ice-carved balustrade as I watched the scene unfold below. The throne room was magnificent in the way that only absolute power could create—walls of living ice that pulsed with inner light, a ceiling that showed the aurora borealis in perpetual motion, and at the center of it all, the Throne of Winter itself.

Carved from a single massive diamond and wreathed in eternal frost, the throne had been my birthright. Should have been my inheritance. Instead, it was occupied by a figure whose face I couldn't quite see, whose presence filled the vast chamber with cold that had nothing to do with ice magic and everything to do with the absence of mercy.

"The boy grows too powerful," a voice said—Chancellor Arcturus, though younger, his silver hair still carrying streaks of black. "The bloodline magic manifests stronger in each generation. If we allow him to reach maturity..."

"He's seven years old," another voice protested, and my heart clenched as I recognized Master Wynne. Even in dreams, even knowing how this ended, part of me hoped the outcome might be different. "He's a child who needs guidance, not... whatever you're proposing."

"He's a threat," a third voice interjected, cold and calculating. In the dream, I could never see the speaker's face clearly, but I knew the voice belonged to someone whose power rivaled the throne itself. "Prince Elian's magic responded to the coronation attempt when he was five. Five years old, and he nearly shattered every ward in the palace. What happens when he's fifteen? Twenty?"

The figure on the throne leaned forward, and though I couldn't see their face, I felt the weight of their attention like ice shards against my skin. "And what of King Boreas? The boy's father grows... unstable. His dreams of magical collaboration, of alliances with the other courts..."

"Are dangerous fantasies that threaten everything we've built," Chancellor Arcturus finished. "The isolation protocols have kept us safe for three centuries. The king's desire to 'restore the ancient ways' will destroy us all."

The ancient ways. Even in the dream, the phrase resonated with significance I was only now beginning to understand. My father had believed in collaboration, in the kind of magical partnerships that Fiona and I were unconsciously recreating.

The scene shifted, as dreams do, and suddenly I was watching my father's last day. Not as the seven-year-old who had been hurried away by loyal servants, but with the understanding of someone who had spent years piecing together fragments of truth.

King Boreas stood in his private study, bent over ancient texts that showed partnerships between different magical species. His ice-blue eyes—so like my own—were bright with possibility as he traced diagrams of collaborative spells that had been forbidden for generations.

"It could work, Elian," he said to the empty air, as if I were there to hear him. "The old partnerships, the way magic was meant to flow between willing hearts and complementary powers. We could heal the damage done by centuries of isolation."

He turned to a portrait on the wall—my mother, Queen Crystalline, who had died bringing me into the world. Her painted eyes seemed to glow with their own inner light, and even in the dream, I felt the weight of a love I'd never known except through my father's memories.

"She would have understood," he continued, his voice heavy with longing. "She always said that ice magic was meant to provide structure for other elements to flourish, not to freeze them out entirely. That royal power was meant to lift others up, not hold them down."

The study door burst open, and Chancellor Arcturus entered with a contingent of court guards. But these weren't the ceremonial guards I remembered from childhood—these were the Shattered Veil operatives, their faces hidden behind masks of black ice, their magic radiating menace.

"Your Majesty," Arcturus said, his voice carrying false regret. "I'm afraid the council has voted. Your recent... experiments in collaborative magic have been deemed too dangerous to continue."

My father straightened, and for a moment, I saw the full power of the Winter Crown manifesting around him—not just ice magic, but something deeper, older, more fundamental. The air itself seemed to crystallize in response to his will.

"And what of my son?" he asked quietly.

"Prince Elian will be... protected. Educated in the proper use of his abilities. Guided away from your unfortunate fascination with ancient partnerships."

"You mean imprisoned," my father said flatly. "Broken. Turned into another puppet for your vision of what the Frost Court should be."

The guards moved closer, their weapons wreathed in magic that felt wrong—corrupted ice, twisted into shapes that had nothing to do with creation or protection.

"It doesn't have to end this way, Boreas," Arcturus said, and there was genuine sadness in his voice that somehow made everything worse. "Abdicate. Accept exile. Let the boy grow up safely away from court politics, and we'll leave you both in peace."

My father's laugh was sharp as breaking crystal. "You and I both know that's a lie. The bloodline magic will manifest whether I'm here or not. And when it does, you'll come for him."

"Then you've made your choice."

The dream blurred, showing flashes of violence that my seven-year-old self had been spared witnessing. Ice magic turned to weapon, trusted advisors revealed as enemies, a throne room that ran red with the blood of those who had tried to protect their king.

When the scene cleared, I was watching from the servants' passage as Master Wynne carried my small, unconscious form toward a hidden portal. My tutor's face was streaked with tears and blood, his usually kind eyes hard with protective fury.

"Remember," he whispered to my sleeping form, "magic is meant to connect, not control. Love is stronger than fear. And someday, when you're ready, you'll find someone whose power complements yours so perfectly that together you can heal what we've broken."

The portal flared to life, showing glimpses of the safe houses and hidden refuges that would become my childhood. But as Master Wynne stepped toward it, Chancellor Arcturus appeared behind him.

"The boy goes," the Chancellor said quietly. "But you... you've filled his head with too many dangerous ideas about collaboration and partnership. You're a liability now."

"He's just a child—"

"He's a prince with the most powerful bloodline magic we've seen in five generations. And thanks to your teaching, he believes that magic should be used for connection rather than control." Arcturus's pale eyes were sad but implacable. "We can't risk him growing up to repeat his father's mistakes."

Master Wynne didn't resist as the guards took him. He just looked once more at my sleeping form and whispered, "Find your partner, little prince. Find the one who makes your magic sing with joy instead of duty. And remember that everything worthwhile is dangerous."

Everything worthwhile is dangerous. The phrase that would become my motto with Fiona, spoken by the man who had taught me that magic could be beautiful instead of merely powerful.

The dream shattered as it always did, and I woke gasping in my chamber at the top of Frost Tower. Dawn light filtered through the crystal walls, painting everything in shades of rose and gold that reminded me painfully of Fiona's magic.

But this time, instead of the familiar weight of grief and guilt, I felt something else: understanding.

My father hadn't died because he was weak or foolish. He had died because he had envisioned exactly what Fiona and I were building together—a partnership that transcended the artificial barriers between magical types, that proved collaboration was stronger than isolation.

And Master Wynne hadn't disappeared because he was a liability. He had been eliminated because he had taught me to believe in the very thing the Shattered Veil feared most: the idea that love and trust could create magic more powerful than fear and control.

Find your partner, he had said. *Find the one who makes your magic sing with joy instead of duty.*

I thought about Fiona, asleep in Shifter Lodge, probably dreaming of reindeer flight patterns or advanced magical theory. I thought about the way our magic flowed together like two halves of a song, about her fierce loyalty and stubborn courage, about the way she looked at me like I was someone worth fighting for rather than a political asset to be managed.

I found her, I thought to the memory of Master Wynne. *I found my partner. Now what do I do with that gift?*

The answer came with the certainty of morning light: *Everything worthwhile is dangerous. And she is definitely worthwhile.*

But there was something else in the dream's aftermath, something that chilled me more than any nightmare: the knowledge that the Shattered Veil was still out there, still working to prevent exactly what Fiona and I were creating. They had killed my father and disappeared my tutor to stop collaborative magic from returning to the world.

They wouldn't hesitate to eliminate us if they thought we posed the same threat.

As I dressed and prepared for another day of training under constant observation, I made a decision that would have terrified the seven-year-old prince but felt natural to the young man I'd become: I was going to tell Fiona everything.

About my father's vision for magical collaboration. About Master Wynne's lessons on partnership and love. About the real reason I'd been hidden away for twenty years, and what forces would align against us if we continued down this path.

She deserved to know what we were really fighting for—and what we were fighting against.

Loving Fiona Prancer—trusting her with my heart, my magic, and my father's dream—was definitely worth the risk.

Even if it meant facing the same forces that had destroyed everyone else I'd ever cared about.

Especially if it meant that.

Because this time, I wouldn't be facing them alone.

CHAPTER ELEVEN
SECRETS AND SPARKS

FIONA

I found Elian in the Frost Tower's observatory, a crystalline dome at the very top of the building that offered a three-hundred-sixty-degree view of the campus. He stood with his back to me, hands clasped behind him as he gazed out at the aurora-painted sky, but something was different about his posture. Less controlled, more weighted down by thoughts that seemed too heavy for someone his age.

The past week had been a blur of intensified training sessions, constant surveillance, and the growing awareness that our enhanced magical connection was changing us in ways neither of us fully understood. My hypersensitive magical senses could feel him from three floors away now—his emotional state, his magical energy levels, even the particular way his power resonated when he was deep in thought.

Today, that resonance carried an undertone of melancholy mixed with something else—determination, maybe, or the aftermath of difficult decisions. The kind of emotional signature that suggested he'd spent the night wrestling with memories he'd rather forget.

"The view from up here is incredible," I said softly, not wanting to startle him.

He turned, and I was struck by how the ethereal light filtering through the crystal walls seemed to illuminate not just his features, but something deeper—a vulnerability that his usual perfect composure never allowed. The magical strain of our recent displays had left its mark on him too. There were faint shadows under his pale eyes, and his silver hair, while still perfectly arranged, seemed to carry frost patterns that shifted with his emotions.

"Fiona." Relief flickered across his features, and through our bond, I felt the way my presence eased something tense and anxious in his chest—but also how that relief was edged with something heavier. "I wasn't sure you'd come looking for me."

"Where else would I go?" I moved to stand beside him, close enough that I could feel the cool energy that always surrounded him, but also close enough to offer the warmth he seemed to crave. Our magical connection settled into harmony automatically, but I could sense undercurrents of unresolved emotion that hadn't been there before. "We're partners, remember? Though you look like you've been wrestling with ghosts all night."

He turned to look at me, and I was struck by something raw in his expression—not just the vulnerability that his usual perfect composure never allowed, but something that looked like the aftermath of old grief, freshly remembered.

"Partners," he repeated, and something in his tone made me look at him more closely. Through our enhanced bond, I could sense layers of meaning in the word—academic partnership, magical collaboration, and something deeper that neither of us had quite found the courage to name.

"You've been thinking," I observed, noting the way frost patterns had formed across the observatory's crystal surfaces in complex, melancholy spirals that seemed to echo whatever he'd been remembering.

"Dangerous habit, I know." The corner of his mouth twitched in what might have been a smile, but his eyes remained distant with the weight of memory. "The dreams came again last night. Stronger this time. More... complete."

Dreams. The way he said it made it clear these weren't ordinary nightmares, but something deeper. More significant.

"About your past?" I asked gently.

Yesterday's training had involved creating a defensive barrier that had held stable for twenty minutes while under sustained magical assault—a feat that should have been impossible for first-year students, according to Professor Hoof's incredulous clipboard notes. The observers had taken extensive readings, and I'd caught at least three different court officials arguing quietly about what our capabilities might mean for "regional stability."

I filled him in on the increased scrutiny, the whispered conferences between officials, and the growing sense that we were being evaluated for purposes that had nothing to do with academics. With each detail, Elian's expression grew more troubled, and the frost patterns on the crystal walls became more agitated.

"And Lysander?" he asked quietly.

"Making friends with people in expensive robes," I replied grimly. "People who ask a lot of questions about our training schedules and magical compatibility assessments."

Elian's hands clenched slightly at his sides, and the temperature in the observatory dropped several degrees. Through our bond, I could feel his anger—not the hot, explosive kind, but the cold, controlled fury of someone who'd learned early that emotional displays could be fatal.

"I should have expected this," he said, his voice carrying a bitterness that made my heart ache. "Nothing good in my life has ever been allowed to remain uncomplicated."

The admission was so raw, so unguarded, that for a moment I forgot about surveillance and politics and the constant pressure we were under. This was just Elian—not the ice prince or the hidden heir, but a young man who'd spent most of his life expecting disappointment.

"Tell me," I said quietly, settling onto the cushioned window seat that curved around part of the observatory. "Tell me what you're really afraid of."

He was quiet for a long moment, his pale eyes distant with memory. When he spoke, his voice carried the weight of grief that had been carefully buried for years.

"When I was seven, I had a tutor named Master Wynne. He was kind to me—the first adult who ever treated me like a child rather than a political asset or liability." Elian's breath misted in the cooling air as old grief surfaced. "He taught me that magic should be joyful, collaborative. That the best spells were created through partnership and trust."

I waited, sensing there was more to the story, and that it wouldn't end well.

"When my guardian discovered our lessons, Master Wynne disappeared. Just... gone. I never saw him again." The frost patterns on the walls had become jagged, painful to look at. "I was told that trusting too easily, caring too much, would get both me and anyone I cared about killed."

Guardian. Not parent, not teacher. Guardian. The word suggested someone who'd had authority over him, but not necessarily love.

"Who was your guardian?" I asked carefully.

"Someone who believed that isolation was safety, that

emotional connections were weaknesses to be exploited." His jaw tightened slightly. "Someone who spent thirteen years teaching me that the only way to survive was to expect nothing from anyone, to trust no one completely."

The weight of his confession settled between us like a physical presence. Through our bond, I could feel the way that lesson had shaped him—the careful distance he maintained, the walls he'd built to protect both himself and others from the consequences of caring.

"I spent thirteen years after that learning to be alone. Learning to expect nothing from anyone, to trust no one completely." His pale eyes met mine, and I saw decades of loneliness reflected there. "And then I came here. And I met you."

My throat tightened with emotion. "Elian..."

"You made me remember what Master Wynne taught me—that magic is supposed to be about connection, about finding someone whose power complements yours so perfectly that together you can create things neither of you could achieve alone." He moved closer, close enough that I could see the flecks of silver in his ice-blue eyes. "You made me want to trust again. You made me remember what it feels like when magic recognizes something it had been looking for."

The phrase echoed between us—the same words I'd used weeks ago to describe that first moment of recognition in the courtyard. But now they carried so much more weight, encompassing not just magical compatibility but emotional truth.

"But?" I prompted, hearing the hesitation in his voice and sensing through our bond that there were deeper truths he was still wrestling with.

"But I remember what happened to Master Wynne. And I wonder if caring about you is going to put you in the same kind of danger." He paused, his expression growing troubled. "There are things about my background, about why I'm really here at NPU, that make our partnership... politically complicated."

Politically complicated. The careful phrasing suggested depths I was only beginning to glimpse.

"You don't have to tell me everything today," I said quietly. "But Elian, whatever your background is, whatever brought you here—I'm not afraid of complicated. I'm afraid of losing what we've built together."

The fear in his voice was so raw it made my chest ache. I stood up from the window seat and moved to face him directly, close enough that our magical auras were overlapping, creating those familiar golden and silver spirals in the air between us.

"Look at me," I said firmly. "Really look at me."

He did, and through our enhanced bond, I opened myself completely—let him feel not just my emotions, but my determination, my certainty, my complete lack of fear about the path we were walking together.

"I'm not Master Wynne," I said quietly. "I'm not going anywhere. Whatever comes, we face it together."

"You don't understand what you're saying. The people who want to use or eliminate our partnership—they have resources, power, influence that—"

"That what? That it scares me, giving up the most important thing that's ever happened to me?" I stepped closer, close enough that I could feel his breath against my cheek. "Elian, before I met you, I was terrified of my own shadow. Terrified I'd never be good enough, never live up to my family's expectations, never find my own path."

The golden light around my hands was growing brighter, responding to the intensity of my emotions. "You didn't just awaken magical abilities I didn't know I had. You awakened *me*. The person I was meant to be."

His breath caught, and through our bond, I felt the moment his careful control began to crack. Not with anger or fear, but with hope—dangerous, beautiful hope that maybe, just maybe, this time would be different.

"Everything worthwhile is dangerous," I said, echoing the words that had become our touchstone. "But Elian, what we have —it's not just worthwhile. It's extraordinary. And I'd rather die fighting for something extraordinary than live safely with something ordinary."

"I can't lose you," he whispered, and the vulnerability in his voice made my heart clench. "Not after finding you. Not after learning what it feels like to have someone understand my magic completely."

"Then don't lose me," I replied simply. "Choose to trust that I'm strong enough to handle whatever consequences come from caring about you. Choose to believe that together, we're more powerful than whatever forces want to tear us apart."

What we might become together, I thought, remembering his words from that first conversation in the library when everything had seemed impossible. Now, standing here with magic spiraling around us and love finally acknowledged between us, I understood what he'd seen even then—not just magical potential, but the possibility of transformation. Of becoming more than either of us could be alone.

For a long moment, we stood there in the crystal observatory, surrounded by the aurora borealis and the visible manifestation of our magical bond. The frost patterns on the walls had transformed from jagged pain into something beautiful—spiraling mandalas that seemed to tell the story of trust chosen over fear, connection chosen over isolation.

"I've never trusted anyone the way I trust you," Elian said finally, and I could feel him making a conscious choice to embrace the risk rather than retreat from it. "It terrifies me and thrills me in equal measure."

"Good," I said with a smile. "That means it matters."

He reached up to touch my face, his fingertips cool against my cheek but carrying warmth beneath the surface. "I love you," he said quietly, and this time the admission didn't seem to surprise him. "Not just your magic, not just the way we fit together in training. I love your courage, your determination, your complete inability to back down from a challenge."

The words hit me like a physical force, sending golden light spiraling through the observatory in patterns that matched the rhythm of my suddenly racing heart. "I love you too," I said, and felt the truth of it resonate through our bond until the very air around us sang with harmony.

When he kissed me, it was with the desperate intensity of someone who'd spent too long afraid to want anything. The magical reaction was immediate and overwhelming—golden and silver light exploding around us, frost patterns racing across every surface, the aurora borealis above us intensifying until the entire observatory blazed with color.

But this time, instead of the chaotic overflow we'd experienced before, our magic wove together in perfect synchronization. Not just compatibility, but true partnership—two halves of something greater, finally allowing themselves to be complete.

When we broke apart, breathless and dizzy from the magical intensity, the observatory had been transformed. Every crystal surface showed images of our shared magical future—not visions of destruction or political chaos, but scenes of creation, collaboration, and the healing of ancient divisions between magical traditions.

"Well," Elian said, his voice rough with emotion and lingering magical resonance, "I suppose subtlety is no longer an option."

I laughed, giddy with relief and power and the simple joy of finally admitting what we both felt. "When has anything about our partnership been subtle?"

"Fair point." He pulled me closer, and I could feel our magical connection settling into a new configuration—deeper, stronger, permanent in ways that went beyond academic assignment or political necessity. "Though I suspect this is going to complicate things considerably."

Through the crystal walls, I could see movement on the campus below—figures in formal robes moving with purpose, their attention focused on the light show we'd just created. Our declaration of love hadn't gone unnoticed, and judging by the speed of their response, it wasn't being received as a romantic gesture.

"Let them come," I said, surprising myself with the fierceness in my voice. "Whatever they're planning, whatever threats they want to make, they're too late. This isn't just a partnership anymore—it's a bond. And bonds like this don't break easily."

Elian's smile was brilliant, carrying none of his usual careful restraint. "No," he agreed, "they don't."

As figures began converging on Frost Tower from multiple directions, I felt not fear but anticipation. Because for the first time since this whole impossible journey began, Elian was choosing trust over the isolation he'd been taught was safety. He was choosing to believe that what we'd built together was worth whatever risks came with it.

We were exactly what we'd been meant to be from the moment our names appeared together on that crystal board: partners in every sense of the word, ready to face whatever came next with the combined strength of magic and love.

Everything worthwhile is dangerous, I thought, understanding now that this had been Master Wynne's final gift to his student—

not just a philosophy, but permission to choose connection despite the cost. *And this is definitely worthwhile.*

But as Elian pulled me closer, his expression growing serious as the sound of approaching voices echoed up the tower stairs, I knew that the deeper truths—about his identity, about the forces that had shaped his life, about the real scope of what we were up against—were still waiting to be shared.

"When this is over," he said quietly, "when we've dealt with whatever this latest crisis brings, I have more to tell you. Things that will help you understand why our partnership is about more than just magical compatibility."

"I'll be ready," I promised, and meant it completely.

The question was whether we'd have the chance for those deeper truths, or whether the forces gathering outside Frost Tower would force revelations before either of us was prepared.

But looking at Elian, seeing the love and determination that had replaced his fear, feeling the absolute certainty of our bond humming beneath my skin, I thought we might just be strong enough to handle whatever truths were coming.

Whether we were ready for them or not.

But it was the sudden flare of crimson light outside the observatory that made my blood run cold.

High above the campus, a burning sigil had appeared in the aurora-painted sky—the ancient symbol of the Order of the Shattered Veil. As we watched, the symbol pulsed once, twice, then began to descend slowly toward Frost Tower like a falling star of judgment.

"They're not coming to talk," Elian said quietly, his voice carrying the lethal calm that meant his royal training was taking over.

Below us, the tower's main entrance burst open with a sound like breaking crystal. A figure in midnight-black robes stepped through the doorway, moving with fluid grace despite the obvious magical restraints built into the building. As frost patterns raced away from their footsteps, I caught a glimpse of eyes that burned with cold fire beneath a raised hood.

The Order of the Shattered Veil had come to claim us.

CHAPTER TWELVE
MAGICAL MISHAP

ELIAN

The morning training session started like any other, but I could sense something different in Fiona's magical signature before we even began. There was an underlying tension, a restless energy that made her golden magic flicker unpredictably around the edges.

"Everything alright?" I asked as we took our positions in the practice arena. The Order of the Shattered Veil's visit three days ago had left both of us on edge, though we hadn't spoken directly about what their cryptic warnings might mean.

"Fine," she replied, but I could hear the strain in her voice. "Just tired. I didn't sleep well."

Neither had I. The dreams had been coming more frequently—memories of the Frost Court, fragments of my father's final days, Master Wynne's disappearance. But more than that, I'd been wrestling with the growing certainty that my carefully maintained anonymity was crumbling. The Order knew who I was. How long before others did as well?

Professor Hoof approached with her ever-present clipboard, her expression mixing encouragement with the kind of focused attention that meant today's exercise would be challenging.

"Advanced barrier construction," she announced. "Today we're working on multi-layered defenses that can adapt to different types of magical attacks. Miss Prancer, you'll be providing the flexibility and responsiveness. Mr. Frost, you'll anchor the structure with precision and stability."

I nodded, already reaching for my magic. The familiar chill spread through my hands as ice began to spiral outward in geometric patterns. But as I started to establish the framework for our barrier, I felt Fiona's magic surge toward mine with unusual intensity.

Something was wrong.

Her golden energy, normally warm and steady, crackled with chaotic undercurrents that spoke of emotional turmoil barely held in check. When our magic touched, instead of the harmonious blending we'd grown accustomed to, there was a jarring discord that made my teeth ache.

"Fiona," I said quietly, not wanting to draw Professor Hoof's attention. "Pull back a little. Your energy is—"

"I know what I'm doing," she snapped, pouring more power into the connection.

But she didn't know. I could feel it through our bond—the way her magic was responding to fears and anxieties she hadn't voiced aloud. Whatever was driving this intensity, it was pushing her beyond safe limits.

The barrier we were attempting to create began to destabilize. What should have been smooth walls of crystallized light became jagged, unpredictable formations that pulsed with barely contained energy. Other students in the practice arena began to back away as the magical pressure built to dangerous levels.

"Miss Prancer," Professor Hoof called out, her voice sharp with concern. "Reduce your output. Your signature is becoming erratic."

"I can handle it," Fiona replied through gritted teeth, but I could see sweat beading on her forehead despite the cold. Her magic was spiraling beyond her control, feeding on itself in a feedback loop that grew stronger with each passing second.

That's when I realized what was about to happen. The chaotic energy building in our shared construct wasn't just going to collapse—it was going to explode outward, taking Fiona's magical channels with it. I'd seen magical burnout before, during my tutoring sessions in the Frost Court. The damage could be permanent.

Without conscious thought, I abandoned the barrier exercise entirely and threw every ounce of my power into containment. Ice erupted around us in a perfect sphere, not to create but to absorb —drawing the chaotic golden energy into crystalline structures that could handle the overflow without harm.

The magical pressure that had been building toward catastrophe suddenly had somewhere to go. Fiona's out-of-control magic flowed into my ice constructs, the chaotic energy transforming into something beautiful as it found proper channels and support.

For a moment, the entire practice arena was filled with a dome of light and ice that sang with harmonic resonance. Then, as quickly as it had begun, the crisis was over. The ice dissolved, the excess energy dissipated, and Fiona collapsed to her knees, breathing hard but unharmed.

"Remarkable," Professor Hoof breathed, making rapid notes on her clipboard. "I've never seen magical overflow redirected so smoothly. Mr. Frost, that was exceptional crisis management."

But I barely heard her praise. All my attention was focused on

Fiona, who was staring at me with an expression of wonder mixed with something that might have been gratitude.

"You saved me," she said quietly, once the other students had dispersed and we were relatively alone in the practice space.

"I did what any partner would do," I replied, though we both knew that wasn't entirely true. What I'd done required not just technical skill, but complete trust in our magical compatibility. I'd opened my power completely to hers, accepting the risk that her chaotic energy might destabilize my own carefully controlled magic.

"No," she said, standing up with only a slight tremor in her legs. "You trusted me. Even when my magic was out of control, even when I could have hurt you, you trusted that we could work together to fix it."

The simple statement hit me with unexpected force. Because she was right—I had trusted her, instinctively and completely, in a way I'd been trained never to trust anyone.

"Fiona," I started, then stopped, unsure how to explain the realization that was taking shape in my mind.

"What was that about?" she asked. "The magical overload, I mean. I've never lost control like that before."

I studied her face, seeing the exhaustion and confusion she was trying to hide. "Fear," I said simply. "Magical energy responds to emotional state. When you're anxious or afraid, it can become chaotic."

"I'm not afraid," she said automatically, then paused. "Or... maybe I am. The Order's visit, the things they implied about your background, the feeling that everything is about to change..."

She trailed off, but I could feel the truth of it through our bond. She was afraid—not of physical danger, but of the unknown. Of losing the partnership we'd built, of discoveries that might change everything between us.

"Change isn't always bad," I said carefully, though the words felt inadequate for the weight of what we were both sensing.

"Isn't it?" She looked at me directly, and I saw vulnerability in her eyes that she rarely allowed others to see. "Elian, I can feel that you're hiding something important. Something that the Order's visit brought closer to the surface. I know you said you needed time but I'm terrified that when I finally learn what it is, it's going to destroy this."

She gestured between us, encompassing not just our magical partnership but the deeper connection that had been growing despite all our careful boundaries.

The honesty in her voice made something crack inside my chest. Here was someone offering trust even while acknowledging fear, choosing connection despite uncertainty. Everything I'd been taught about emotional vulnerability being weakness seemed suddenly, utterly wrong.

"It might," I admitted, and saw her flinch slightly. "But Fiona, whatever changes are coming, we'll face them together. That's what partners do."

"Promise?" she asked, and the simple word carried the weight of everything we hadn't yet said to each other.

"Promise," I replied, meaning it completely despite the political complications I couldn't yet share.

As we gathered our training equipment and prepared to leave the practice arena, I felt something fundamental shift in the dynamic between us. The magical crisis had forced us past another barrier—not just of technique, but of trust. She'd shown me her vulnerability, and I'd responded by protecting rather than exploiting it.

For someone raised in the calculated world of court politics, the experience was both terrifying and exhilarating.

"Same time tomorrow?" Fiona asked as we reached the exit.

"Always," I replied, and realized that the word carried new meaning now. Not just a commitment to training schedules, but a promise that whatever revelations lay ahead, we would face them as partners.

The real test would be whether that promise could survive the truth about who I really was, and what loving me might cost her.

But walking across campus with Fiona beside me, feeling the settled harmony of our magical bond after the morning's crisis, I allowed myself to hope that maybe—just maybe—trust and partnership could prove stronger than the political forces that had shaped my entire life.

After all, she'd already proven that she was willing to fight for what we were building together.

The question was whether I was brave enough to give her something worth fighting for.

CHAPTER THIRTEEN
A SNOW SPRITE'S WARNING

FIONA

The snow sprite appeared in my dormitory window three nights after the training mishap, her gossamer wings leaving trails of ice crystals as she hovered anxiously outside the glass. At first, I thought she might be lost—sprites rarely ventured this close to the main campus buildings, preferring the wild spaces at the forest's edge.

But when I opened the window, she darted inside with the desperate urgency of someone carrying important news.

"Fiona Prancer," she said in a voice like wind chimes made of ice, "I bring warning from the deep forest. The ancient magics stir. The old pathways wake. Danger comes on winter's breath."

I blinked, still half-asleep and struggling to process what she was saying. "I'm sorry, what? Slow down—what kind of danger?"

The sprite, no bigger than my hand, perched on my windowsill and wrapped her translucent wings around herself like a cloak. Her silver hair seemed to move in a breeze that touched nothing else in the room, and her pale blue eyes held the kind of ancient wisdom that reminded me uncomfortably of the oldest professors at NPU.

"The storms gather strength," she continued, her musical voice carrying undertones of genuine fear. "Not natural storms—magical ones. The kind that reshape the boundaries between worlds, that tear holes in the fabric of reality itself."

"Magical storms?" I sat up fully, sleep forgotten. "Where? When?"

"Soon. The signs are everywhere for those who know how to read them." She gestured toward my window, where frost patterns had been appearing more frequently since Elian and I had started training together. "Your magic calls to his, yes? Fire and ice, warmth and crystal, two halves of an ancient song?"

"How do you know about that?" I asked, though something about her presence felt familiar in a way I couldn't quite place.

"The sprites have been watching. We remember the old partnerships, from before the courts built walls between the magical peoples. We remember what happens when such bonds awaken." Her expression grew troubled. "But we also remember what comes hunting when the old power stirs."

A chill ran down my spine that had nothing to do with the winter air flowing through the open window. "What comes hunting?"

"Those who feast on disruption. Those who grow strong when the careful balance is broken." She flew closer, her tiny features creased with worry. "They sense the change in you and your ice prince. They know that what you are becoming together could either heal the ancient wounds or tear them wider."

Ice prince. The casual way she said it made my heart skip a beat. "What do you mean, ice prince?"

"You do not know?" The sprite's eyes widened with what

looked like genuine surprise. "Oh, child. The danger is greater than we thought, if he has not yet trusted you with the truth."

"What truth?" I demanded, but she was already backing toward the window, her wings catching the moonlight like captured starlight.

"That is not my secret to share. But know this—the storm that comes will test more than your magical abilities. It will test your bond, your trust, your willingness to stand together when all the world seeks to tear you apart." She paused at the windowsill, looking back with eyes that seemed far too old for her delicate features. "The sprites have survived many such storms. We know the signs. And we know that some partnerships are worth preserving, no matter the cost."

"Wait," I called out, but she was already gone, disappearing into the night like a fragment of winter dream.

I sat in my dormitory room for a long time after she left, staring at the frost patterns on my window and trying to make sense of what she'd told me. Magical storms. Ancient partnerships. Something was hunting us because of what we were becoming together.

And underneath it all, the nagging certainty that Elian was hiding something significant—something that even the sprites of the deep forest knew, but I did not. Not for sure.

The next morning brought confirmation that the sprite's warnings weren't just folklore and superstition. I woke to find the entire campus covered in a thin layer of ice that shouldn't have been possible given the weather patterns. More unsettling, the ice formed intricate patterns that seemed to radiate outward from specific points—the training grounds where Elian and I practiced, the library where we studied together, even the path between Shifter Lodge and Frost Tower.

"It's like a map," Brynn observed as we made our way carefully across the slippery courtyard toward breakfast. "A map of your magical connection with Elian."

She was right, and the implications made my stomach clench with anxiety. If our bond was becoming visible to anyone who knew how to look, how long before it attracted the kind of attention we weren't prepared to handle?

"Has anything like this happened before?" I asked Professor Hoof during Advanced Flight Theory, gesturing toward the ice patterns that were still visible outside the classroom windows despite the morning sun.

"Not in my experience," she replied, her expression troubled as she studied the crystalline formations. "Though there are historical accounts of similar phenomena during periods of magical... instability."

"What kind of instability?"

"The kind that precedes significant changes in the magical world. New alliances forming, old boundaries shifting, power dynamics that have been stable for generations suddenly becoming fluid." She looked at me directly, and I had the uncomfortable feeling that she knew exactly why I was asking. "The kind of instability that makes certain parties very nervous."

The morning training session with Elian did nothing to ease my growing anxiety. If anything, our magical connection seemed stronger and more volatile than ever. Every time our power touched, the air around us shimmered with visible energy, and I could swear I heard something like distant music in the harmony of our combined abilities.

"Are you feeling it too?" I asked as we worked through a complex collaborative spell that should have been well within our abilities but was producing effects far beyond what we'd intended.

"The... intensity?" Elian paused in his movements, ice crystals still spiraling around his hands in patterns that were almost hypnotically beautiful. "Yes. It's as if something is amplifying our natural compatibility."

"The sprite said something was coming. Something that hunts partnerships like ours."

He went very still, his magical signature flickering with what felt like fear quickly suppressed. "What sprite?"

I told him about the midnight visit, about the warnings and the cryptic references to ice princes and ancient partnerships. As I spoke, I watched his expression grow increasingly troubled, though he tried to hide his reaction.

"Sprites are... perceptive," he said carefully when I finished. "They're connected to the oldest magical currents in ways that more civilized species sometimes forget."

"Elian," I said, moving closer so we couldn't be overheard by other students, "what aren't you telling me? The sprite acted like she knew something about you, something important that I should know too."

For a moment, I thought he might actually answer. I could see the internal struggle playing out across his features—the desire to trust warring against whatever had taught him that secrets were safer than honesty.

But then Professor Hoof called out that training time was over, and the moment passed.

"Later," he said quietly. "When we have privacy and time to discuss... complicated things."

That evening, I found myself in the Enchanted Library, researching everything I could find about magical storms and ancient partnerships. The texts I discovered were fragmentary and often contradictory, but they painted a picture of magical history that was far more turbulent than anything we'd been taught in standard courses.

There had been other partnerships like ours—bonds between different magical species that transcended normal compatibility. But they had also attracted attention from forces that saw such connections as either opportunities to exploit or threats to eliminate.

The Sundering Wars of the Third Age, one particularly old text noted, *began when collaborative partnerships grew strong enough to challenge the established court hierarchies. The response was swift and brutal—systematic elimination of mixed-species bonds through political pressure, magical suppression, and when necessary, direct violence.*

I was so absorbed in my reading that I almost missed the soft footsteps approaching my table. When I looked up, I found a figure in midnight-blue robes standing nearby—not a student, but someone whose presence made the very air around them seem colder.

"Miss Prancer," the figure said, lowering their hood to reveal sharp features and eyes like chips of winter sky. "How fortuitous to find you here. I believe we need to have a conversation."

"I'm sorry, do I know you?" I asked, though something about their magical signature felt familiar in an unsettling way.

"Not yet. But you know someone who is very important to me. Someone who has been... less than forthcoming about his true circumstances." The stranger smiled, and it held no warmth whatsoever. "Someone who may have forgotten that royal blood carries obligations that transcend personal preferences."

Royal blood. The words hit me like ice water, confirming the sprite's cryptic warnings in the worst possible way.

"I think there's been a misunderstanding," I began, but the stranger held up a hand for silence.

"Elian has been permitted considerable latitude in his educational pursuits," they continued as if I hadn't spoken. "But recent... developments suggest that his partnership with you is becoming problematic. We thought it best to speak with you directly about the situation."

"Who is *we*?" I demanded, though my voice came out smaller than I'd intended.

"People who have spent considerable effort keeping the prince safe and anonymous. People who are concerned that his growing attachment to you may compromise that safety." The stranger leaned forward slightly, and I caught the scent of winter wind and old magic. "People who are prepared to take whatever steps are necessary to preserve the delicate balance that has protected him for twenty years."

The threat was subtle but unmistakable. They weren't just warning me about dangers that might come—they were the danger, prepared to eliminate whatever they saw as a threat to their carefully laid plans.

"What do you want?" I asked.

"For now? Simply awareness. You are involved in something far more complex and dangerous than you realize, Miss Prancer. Forces are aligning that could destroy not just your partnership, but everything and everyone you care about." They pulled their hood back up, preparing to leave. "Consider carefully whether your feelings for the prince are worth such consequences."

After they left, I sat alone in the library for a long time, the ancient texts forgotten as I tried to process what had just happened. Elian wasn't just hiding his past—he was hiding his identity as royalty, apparently from people who had been protecting him through concealment and isolation.

And now our growing partnership was threatening that protection.

The sprite had been right. The storm was coming, and it would test more than our magical abilities. It would test whether love and trust could survive the kind of political pressure that had apparently been building around us for months without my knowledge.

But even as fear twisted in my stomach, I felt something else rising to meet it: determination. Whatever secrets Elian was carrying, whatever forces were aligning against us, I wasn't going to let them tear apart the best thing that had ever happened to me without a fight.

The question was whether I was strong enough for the battle that was coming, and whether Elian would trust me enough to fight it together.

As I gathered my books and prepared to return to Shifter Lodge, I noticed that new frost patterns had appeared on the library windows while I'd been reading—not random crystalline formations, but symbols that looked almost like writing. A message, perhaps, or a warning.

Either way, the magical storm the sprite had predicted was definitely gathering strength.

And I had the sinking feeling that tomorrow would bring the kind of revelations that would change everything between Elian and me, whether we were ready for them or not.

CHAPTER FOURTEEN
FOREST TRIAL

ELIAN

The decision to accept Professor Hoof's "optional extra credit exercise" in the Enchanted Forest had been mine, though I was beginning to question that choice as we entered our third hour of what should have been a simple navigation challenge.

The forest was rearranging itself around us.

Paths appeared and disappeared, clearings shifted position when we weren't looking directly at them, and the compass readings made no sense whatsoever. More unsettling, I could feel the ancient magic of this place pressing against my consciousness, demanding something I wasn't ready to give.

Truth, the forest seemed to whisper with every step we took deeper into its heart. *No more secrets. No more hiding.*

Beside me, Fiona moved with increasing tension, her magical signature flickering with the anxiety that had been building since her mysterious library encounter two nights ago. She'd tried to tell me about it—someone in blue robes, veiled threats about

Prince Elian, warnings about forces aligning against us. But every time she'd mentioned the title, I'd deflected the conversation.

I was running out of deflections.

"This isn't normal," she said as we emerged from yet another path that definitely hadn't existed when we'd entered it twenty minutes earlier. "Forests don't reorganize themselves for the convenience of lost students."

"No," I agreed, pausing to study the trees around us. Ancient oaks whose bark shifted between silver and deep green, their branches intertwining overhead in patterns that reminded me uncomfortably of the throne room back home. "They don't. Which means this isn't really about navigation."

"Then what is it about?"

I looked at her—really looked at her. Auburn hair catching the filtered sunlight, green eyes bright with intelligence and frustration, magical energy spiraling around her hands in agitated patterns that spoke of questions she was tired of not asking.

She deserved the truth. She'd earned it through weeks of partnership, through trust offered even when I hadn't reciprocated, through loyalty that had never wavered despite my obvious evasions.

But giving her the truth would change everything between us. It would put her in danger. It would make her a target for people who had already proven they would kill to maintain their version of stability.

"It's about confronting the things we're afraid to face," I said finally, settling onto a fallen log that was carved with symbols I recognized as ancient Frost Court sigils. "The forest responds to emotional and magical resonance. It creates challenges based on what it senses we need to resolve."

"And what does it sense we need to resolve?" she asked, though her tone suggested she suspected the answer.

The question hung in the air between us like a sword waiting to fall. Around us, the forest had gone utterly still—no wind in the branches, no sound of distant birds, even the usual magical hum reduced to expectant silence.

Twenty years of careful anonymity had led to this moment. Twenty years of assumed identities, manufactured histories, and emotional walls designed to keep people at a safe distance. All of it was about to crumble because I'd been foolish enough to fall in love with someone whose magic called to mine with perfect harmony.

"Each other," I said quietly. "Our fears. The secrets we've been carrying."

As if summoned by my words, the clearing around us began to transform. The carved log we sat on revealed more complex symbols—not just Frost Court sigils, but genealogical markers that traced royal bloodlines back through centuries. The trees rearranged themselves into a circle, their branches forming a natural cathedral that felt sacred and somehow final.

"Elian," Fiona said, her voice carefully controlled, "who are you really?"

The simple question carried the weight of everything we'd built together and everything we stood to lose. I could feel her magical signature reaching toward mine, not demanding but offering—willing to accept whatever truth I was finally ready to share.

"My name," I said, the words feeling strange and rustic after so many years of careful lies, "is Prince Elian Frostborn. Heir to the Throne of Winter and rightful king of the Frost Court."

She went very still, her magical signature flickering with shock that quickly transformed into understanding. Pieces of a puzzle falling into place—my unconscious authority, my advanced magical training, the way court officials spoke to me, the political implications that had been swirling around our partnership.

"Prince," she repeated faintly. "As in... actual royalty."

"As in my father was King Boreas of the Frost Court, murdered by his own council when I was seven years old because he believed in exactly what you and I have been creating together—collaborative magic between different species."

The grief in my voice was older than our partnership, older than my time at NPU, older than most of my conscious memories. But speaking it aloud to someone who might understand felt like lancing a wound that had been festering for decades.

"King Boreas," she said, her voice soft with recognition. "I've heard stories... the Frost King who died under mysterious circumstances."

"Not mysterious to those who killed him." The bitterness in my voice surprised even me. "He wanted to restore the ancient partnerships, to tear down the barriers that kept magical species isolated from each other. The council saw that as a threat to their power, to the careful hierarchies they'd spent centuries building."

Through our bond, I could feel her processing not just the political implications but the personal cost. A seven-year-old child losing everything in a single night—father, home, identity, future—all because of beliefs that now seemed prophetic rather than dangerous.

"That's why you've been hiding," she said with growing understanding. "Not just from casual discovery, but from people who would kill you for what you represent."

"Among other things, yes." I moved closer, needing her to understand that this wasn't just ancient history but ongoing danger. "Fiona, the people who murdered my father—they're still in power. They've spent twenty years believing that collaborative magic died with him, that the threat he represented was eliminated."

"But it wasn't," she realized. "Because you're here. Because we're here, proving that everything he believed was possible."

"Exactly. And now that our partnership is attracting attention, now that people are starting to notice what we can accomplish together..." I paused, studying her face for signs of the fear that should have been there. Instead, I saw determination mixed with something that looked like fierce protectiveness. "They're going to want to eliminate the threat before it can grow."

"Let them try," she said with such quiet conviction that it took my breath away.

"Fiona, you don't understand what you're saying. These aren't academic rivals or political opponents. These are people who orchestrated the murder of a king and covered it up for two decades. They have resources, influence, power that—"

"That scares me into abandoning the best thing that's ever happened to me?" She stood up, golden light beginning to spiral around her hands with increasing intensity. "Elian, I don't care if you're a prince or a pauper or the secret heir to a magical empire. I care about who you are when we're together—the person who saved me when my magic went out of control, who trusts me with techniques that could be dangerous, who looks at me like I'm someone worth fighting for."

The declaration hit me with the force of summer lightning. Because in twenty years of careful survival, no one had ever chosen me over safety. No one had ever looked at the political complications surrounding my existence and decided they were worth facing.

"Everything worthwhile is dangerous," I said, echoing Master Wynne's words from so long ago.

"Then this is definitely worthwhile," she replied, moving

closer until I could see the flecks of gold in her green eyes that matched the light dancing around her fingers.

But even as relief flooded through me at her acceptance, I could hear sounds in the forest that made my royal training kick into high alert. Something was moving through the underbrush with predatory intent—multiple somethings, by the sound of it.

"We're not alone," I said grimly, ice already beginning to spiral around my hands in defensive patterns.

Fiona's expression sharpened as her enhanced senses picked up what mine had detected. "Frost wolves. Six, maybe seven." She looked around the clearing with new understanding. "Someone put them here. This isn't just a training exercise anymore."

"No," I agreed, recognizing the particular magical signature of creatures that were drawn to powerful mages. "This is a test. To see if we can survive the kind of direct attacks that come with being too dangerous to ignore."

The wolves emerged from the forest in coordinated fashion— creatures the size of horses with fur white as fresh snow and eyes that glowed with predatory intelligence. But these weren't wild animals. These were magical constructs, designed specifically to test collaborative partnerships under lethal pressure.

"Ready?" I asked, ice barriers already forming around us as the pack closed in.

"Ready," she replied, golden fire spiraling around her hands like living weapons.

What followed was less like combat and more like a deadly dance. Where I created structure and defense, she provided flexibility and power. Where her instincts guided us toward openings, my precision ensured we didn't waste energy on futile attacks. Our magic flowed together with such perfect synchronization that the wolves' attempts to separate us only made our bond stronger.

By the time the last construct dissolved into magical energy, the clearing had been transformed into a showcase of collaborative power that neither of us could have achieved alone. Ice and light wove together in patterns so beautiful they seemed to sing, proving beyond any doubt that what my father had died believing was not only possible but inevitable.

"That wasn't random," Fiona said as we stood among the evidence of our victory, both of us glowing faintly with residual magical energy.

"No. That was a demonstration. For whoever sent the wolves, for anyone who's been wondering whether our partnership represents opportunity or threat." I looked around the clearing, at the magnificent and deadly art we'd created without conscious thought. "And I think we just answered that question."

"Are you afraid?" she asked.

I considered the question seriously, taking stock of emotions that had been too dangerous to acknowledge for most of my life. Fear, yes—of discovery, of the political consequences that would follow, of the people who would try to use our bond for their own purposes or destroy it to prevent others from doing the same.

But underneath the fear was something I'd never allowed myself to feel before: hope.

"Terrified," I admitted. "But also... hopeful. For the first time in twenty years, I'm not facing an impossible situation alone."

"Good," she said, moving closer until our magical auras overlapped completely. "Because I have a feeling the impossible is going to be our specialty."

When she kissed me, it was with the fierce intensity of someone who had just chosen to fight for something worth preserving. Our magic exploded around us in patterns of light and ice that painted the entire clearing in silver and gold, but this time the power felt controlled, purposeful, celebratory rather than chaotic.

As we broke apart, breathless and dizzy from both the kiss and the magical intensity, I felt something fundamental shift in my understanding of what was possible. For twenty years, I'd believed that loving someone meant putting them in danger. But standing here with Fiona, feeling the absolute certainty of our bond strengthened rather than threatened by truth, I realized that love might actually be the thing that made survival possible.

"So what happens now?" she asked, her hand still linked with mine as our magic settled into harmony around us.

"Now we prove that collaborative magic is stronger than the forces trying to prevent it," I said, surprised by the confidence in my own voice. "We show them that some partnerships are worth any risk."

And for the first time since I was seven years old, I believed that always might actually be possible.

The journey back to campus would bring new challenges, new pressures, new attempts to tear apart what we'd built. But we would face them with complete honesty between us, with trust that had been tested and proven unbreakable, with magic that sang in perfect harmony.

Everything worthwhile was dangerous. But some things were worth any danger to preserve.

And what Fiona and I had found together was definitely worth fighting for.

CHAPTER FIFTEEN
FALLOUT

FIONA

I woke up the morning after the forest trial with frost patterns covering every surface of my dormitory room.

Not just the windows this time—the walls, the ceiling, even my textbooks were traced with delicate crystalline designs that pulsed with residual magical energy. The patterns were beautiful, intricate, and completely impossible to explain to anyone who might ask.

Prince Elian Frostborn.

The name echoed in my head like a bell that wouldn't stop ringing. Not just Elian, my training partner, who saved me from magical overload and looked at me like I was worth fighting for. Not just the mysterious transfer student who made my magic sing with perfect harmony.

A prince. Actual royalty. Heir to a throne and a kingdom and political responsibilities I couldn't even begin to comprehend.

"Those are new," Brynn observed from her bed, following my gaze to the most elaborate frost pattern I'd ever seen—a mandala covering our entire ceiling that seemed to tell the story of every-thing that had happened in the forest. "And they're... everywhere."

"Unconscious magical manifestation," I said, echoing Elian's explanation from weeks ago. "It happens when powerful emotions destabilize magical control."

"What kind of powerful emotions?" she asked, though her tone suggested she already suspected.

I closed my eyes, remembering the way Elian had looked when he'd finally told me the truth. Vulnerable and terrified and desperate for understanding. The way he'd kissed me after we'd defeated the frost wolves, like I was something precious he'd never expected to find.

The way I'd felt when our magic had flowed together in perfect harmony, creating something neither of us could have achieved alone.

"The complicated kind," I replied, opening my eyes to find Brynn studying me with concern.

"Fiona, what happened in that forest?"

The question hung in the air between us like a challenge. Because how could I explain that in the span of a few hours, everything I'd thought I knew about my partnership with Elian had been turned upside down?

How could I tell her that the person I'd fallen in love with was not just hiding his past, but hiding an identity that came with centuries of political baggage, court intrigue, and enemies who had already proven they would kill to maintain their power?

"He told me who he really is," I said finally. "All of it. The truth he's been carrying for twenty years."

"And?"

"And I have no idea what to do with that information."

I spent the rest of the morning avoiding the places where I

might encounter Elian. Not because I was angry—how could I be angry when he'd trusted me with secrets that could get him killed?—but because I needed space to think without the constant pull of our magical connection influencing my judgment.

The problem was that thinking led to questions I didn't want to answer.

What did it mean to be in love with a prince? Not just the romantic fantasy version, but the reality of political marriages, diplomatic obligations, and a life lived entirely in service to others? What did it mean that our partnership had apparently awakened magic that certain people saw as dangerous enough to eliminate?

What did it mean that I, Fiona Prancer from a perfectly ordinary reindeer shifter family, was now connected to forces that operated on a scale I'd never imagined?

By lunchtime, the questions had multiplied into full-blown panic.

"You're spiraling," Marcus observed as he found me hiding in the furthest corner of the Enchanted Library, surrounded by towers of books about royal protocols and court politics that I wasn't actually reading.

"I'm researching," I corrected, though even I could hear the lack of conviction in my voice.

"You're panicking," he said, settling into the chair across from me with the kind of gentle directness that made him such a good friend. "What's going on, Fiona? Yesterday you were happier than I'd ever seen you, and today you look like you're planning to flee the country."

"Maybe I am," I muttered, then immediately felt guilty for the betrayal implicit in the words.

"Okay, talk to me. What happened?"

I looked around the library, noting the other students within earshot, the way conversations seemed to pause when people noticed me. Even here, I could feel the weight of attention that had been building around my partnership with Elian for weeks.

"Can we go somewhere more private?" I asked.

Twenty minutes later, we were sitting in the winter rose garden where Elian had first shown me vulnerable honesty, where he'd admitted his fears about trusting people and I'd promised to be someone worth trusting in return.

The irony wasn't lost on me.

"He's not just a transfer student," I said without preamble, needing to get the words out before I lost my nerve. "He's Prince Elian Frostborn, heir to the Frost Court throne, and apparently his very existence threatens the political stability that certain people have spent decades maintaining."

Marcus went very still, his snow owl shifter instincts no doubt picking up on the genuine fear underlying my words. "Prince," he repeated carefully. "As in actual royalty."

"As in his father was murdered by his own council for believing in collaborative magic, and Elian has been in hiding for twenty years because those same people would kill him if they discovered he'd inherited both his father's power and his father's ideals."

"And you learned this how?"

"He told me. Yesterday, in the forest, when we were facing down magical constructs that were apparently testing whether our partnership could survive lethal pressure." I laughed, but it came out bitter. "Right before he kissed me and made me believe that maybe, just maybe, we could make this work despite all the complications."

Marcus was quiet for a long moment, processing the magnitude of what I'd just revealed. "That's... significant," he said finally.

"That's terrifying," I corrected. "Marcus, I don't know how to be someone's girlfriend, let alone a prince's girlfriend. I don't know anything about court politics or diplomatic protocols or the kind of life he'll be expected to live."

"Has he asked you to know those things?"

"That's not the point. The point is that loving him means accepting responsibilities I never chose, dangers I'm not prepared for, and a future that looks nothing like anything I've ever imagined for myself."

"And?" Marcus prompted gently.

"And I'm not sure I'm brave enough for that," I admitted, the words feeling like glass in my throat.

"Fiona," Marcus said, leaning forward with the kind of intensity I rarely saw from him, "do you love him?"

The question hit me like a physical blow. Because, of course, I loved him. I loved the way he looked at me like I was someone worth fighting for. I loved his quiet competence, his unexpected vulnerability, his determination to be worthy of his father's legacy. I loved the way our magic flowed together like two halves of a song, and the way he made me feel like the strongest version of myself.

But love didn't make the political implications disappear. Love didn't erase the fact that people had died for believing in the same collaborative magic we were creating together.

"Yes," I said quietly. "I love him completely. Which is exactly why I'm terrified."

"Because you think loving him will put you in danger?"

"Because I think loving him will put everyone I care about in danger. My family, my friends, anyone who gets caught in the crossfire when the people who killed his father decide our partnership has become too threatening to tolerate."

Marcus was quiet for several minutes, studying my face with

the kind of attention that made me feel like he was seeing more than I intended to show.

"You know," he said finally, "I've been watching you and Elian together for months. And the thing that's always struck me isn't how different you are, but how similar. You're both people who've spent most of your lives trying to live up to other people's expectations, trying to be worthy of legacies you inherited rather than chose."

"What's your point?"

"My point is that maybe the reason your magic works so well together isn't just compatibility—it's recognition. You understand each other in ways that most people never will." He paused, studying the frost patterns that were beginning to form on the garden benches around us despite the afternoon sun. "And maybe the reason certain people find your partnership so threatening isn't because it's dangerous, but because it proves that collaboration is stronger than the isolation they've been enforcing."

His words sent a shiver through me that had nothing to do with the temperature. Because he was right, wasn't he? The magic Elian and I created together wasn't chaotic or destructive—it was harmonious, beautiful, proof that different types of power could work together to create something stronger than either could achieve alone.

"But what if I'm not strong enough?" I asked. "What if I can't handle the pressure, the scrutiny, the political implications of being with him?"

"Then you'll figure it out together," Marcus said simply. "That's what partnerships are for."

"And if I get him killed because I'm not smart enough to navigate court politics?"

"Then you'll have tried to build something worth the risk instead of letting fear make your decisions for you."

The simple statement hit me with unexpected force. Because that's what I was doing, wasn't it? Letting fear drive my choices instead of trusting the foundation Elian and I had built together.

But even as I recognized the truth of Marcus's words, I couldn't shake the image of Elian as he'd looked when he'd told me about Master Wynne's disappearance—grief and guilt and the bone-deep certainty that caring about him had gotten someone else hurt.

What if history repeated itself? What if my feelings for him, my magical connection to him, made me a target for people who wanted to use our bond against him?

"I need to think," I said, standing up from the bench. "I need... space to figure out what all of this means."

"Fiona," Marcus called as I started to walk away. "For what it's worth, I think you're stronger than you give yourself credit for. And I think Elian knows that too."

I made it halfway back to Shifter Lodge before I ran into the person I'd been trying to avoid all day.

Elian stood near the fountain in the central courtyard, and even from a distance, I could see the frost patterns spreading outward from where he stood. He looked like he hadn't slept, his usual perfect composure frayed around the edges in a way that spoke of emotional turmoil barely held in check.

When he saw me, relief flickered across his features so quickly I might have imagined it.

"Fiona," he said, moving toward me with careful steps that suggested he wasn't sure of his welcome. "I was hoping we could talk."

"I need time," I said quickly, before he could say something that would make me forget all the very reasonable concerns I'd been wrestling with. "To process everything you told me yesterday. To figure out what it all means."

Something that might have been hurt flashed across his expression, but he nodded with the kind of dignity that reminded me exactly who he was—not just the person I'd fallen in love with, but someone who'd been trained from birth to handle rejection with grace.

"Of course," he said quietly. "Take all the time you need."

But as I walked away, I could feel his gaze following me, could sense through our bond the confusion and growing despair he was trying so hard to hide. He thought I was rejecting him, I realized. He thought that learning the truth about his identity had changed how I felt about him.

Nothing could be further from the truth.

I loved him more now than I had before the forest, because I finally understood the courage it had taken to trust me with secrets that could destroy him. I loved his determination to be worthy of his father's legacy, his willingness to risk everything for the possibility of collaborative magic, his quiet strength in the face of forces that had been trying to break him for twenty years.

But love didn't make the dangers less real. Love didn't change the fact that people had died for the ideals we were unconsciously representing.

That evening, I sat in my dormitory room staring at the frost patterns that continued to spread across every surface despite my attempts to suppress my magical connection to Elian. The designs were getting more complex, more beautiful, and more impossible to explain with each passing hour.

"You can't avoid him forever," Brynn said gently, settling on her bed with a cup of hot chocolate that steamed in the cooling air. "Whatever's going on between you two, it's affecting the entire campus. Professor Hoof mentioned that the training grounds have been experiencing 'unusual atmospheric disturbances' since yesterday."

"I'm not avoiding him," I said, though we both knew that was a lie. "I'm trying to make a rational decision about something that's completely irrational."

"Love usually is."

"This isn't just about love. This is about politics and ancient grudges and people who have already proven they'll kill to maintain their power." I turned away from the window where new frost patterns were forming even as we spoke. "This is about whether I'm willing to put everyone I care about at risk for something that might not even be possible to sustain."

"And what have you decided?"

I closed my eyes, feeling the constant pull of our magical connection like a second heartbeat in my chest. Even with physical distance between us, even with my deliberate attempts to suppress our bond, I could feel Elian's presence like a flame that called to something deep in my magical core.

"I've decided," I said quietly, "that I'm a coward."

"Fiona—"

"No, it's true. I'm choosing safety over possibility, fear over love, because I'm too afraid of what it might cost to fight for something extraordinary." I opened my eyes to find frost spiraling across the ceiling in patterns that looked almost like writing. "And the worst part is that I know I'm hurting him by pulling away, but I don't know how to stop being afraid."

Brynn was quiet for a long moment, studying the magical displays that were turning our dormitory room into a winter wonderland despite my emotional turmoil.

"You know," she said finally, "fear isn't always a bad thing. Sometimes it's what keeps us alive long enough to figure out what's worth the risk."

"And what if what's worth the risk gets other people killed?"

"Then you'll have to decide whether living with that possibility is worse than living with the certainty that you gave up something extraordinary because you were too afraid to try."

Her words followed me into restless sleep, where I dreamed of frost patterns that told stories of partnerships that had changed the world, of love that had proven stronger than the forces trying to destroy it, of choices that echoed through generations long after the people who made them were gone.

When I woke the next morning, there was a letter waiting on my windowsill, written in familiar handwriting on paper that felt like compressed starlight.

Fiona,

I understand your need for space and time to process everything I told you. I also understand if learning the truth about who I am changes how you feel about our partnership.

But I want you to know that whatever you decide, these past months with you have been the best of my life. You made me remember what it feels like to hope for something beyond mere survival. You made me believe that collaborative magic could be beautiful instead of just dangerous.

Most importantly, you made me brave enough to trust someone completely for the first time in twenty years.

Whatever comes next, I will never regret telling you the truth. And I will never regret falling in love with someone who showed me that some things are worth any risk to preserve.

Take all the time you need. I'll be here when you're ready.

Always, Elian

I read the letter three times, tears streaming down my face as the weight of his love and understanding settled around me like armor against my fears.

He wasn't demanding answers or pressuring me to make a decision before I was ready. He was simply offering unconditional love and infinite patience, trusting that whatever I decided would come from a place of honesty rather than fear.

It was, I realized, exactly what I should have expected from someone who'd spent twenty years learning to put other people's well-being before his own desires.

But it was also what finally helped me understand that the real question wasn't whether I was brave enough to love a prince.

The real question was whether I was brave enough to let a prince love me back.

And looking around my frost-covered dormitory room, feeling the constant pull of our magical connection despite all my attempts to suppress it, seeing the evidence of just how fundamental our bond had become to my magical equilibrium, I realized that the choice had already been made.

I couldn't run from this because it was already part of who I was. The only question was whether I would face it with courage or let fear destroy the best thing that had ever happened to me.

Tomorrow I would find Elian and tell him that I was ready to be brave. That I was ready to fight for something extraordinary, even if it scared me more than anything I'd ever faced.

Tonight, I would just sit with the frost patterns and let myself feel everything I'd been trying to suppress: love and fear and determination and the growing certainty that some partnerships were worth any risk to preserve.

Even if that risk included everything I'd ever thought I wanted my future to look like.

CHAPTER SIXTEEN
CONNOR'S WISDOM

ELIAN

The morning after our conversation in the forest felt different. Not just because of what I'd revealed about my identity, but because of the careful distance Fiona had maintained since then. Through our bond, I could sense her processing, weighing, deciding—and the uncertainty was more unsettling than any political pressure I'd faced from the Frost Court.

I was reviewing Advanced Magical Theory notes in the Crystal Dining Hall when I felt her emotional state shift toward something like resolve. Through our connection, I could trace her location as she moved through the building, finally settling somewhere that felt like she was having an important conversation.

She wasn't alone.

The magical signature accompanying her was familiar—Connor Prancer, our fellow freshman who'd somehow managed to balance legendary Christmas Eve flight achievement with the same academic pressures the rest of us faced. Fiona's cousin, the family member who understood the weight of living up to an impossible legacy while trying to figure out your own identity.

I'd seen Connor most mornings at breakfast, usually at his regular table near the windows, often texting someone during the early hours—probably his girlfriend Kayla, who was studying law at Oxford. The time difference meant their conversations happened during our breakfast periods, and I'd noticed how his face would soften whenever her name appeared on his phone.

Now he was talking with Fiona, and through our bond, I felt the conversation's emotional intensity without being able to discern specific words. Fear, uncertainty, hope, determination—a complex weaving of feelings that suggested she was working through everything I'd told her about my true identity and what it meant for our partnership.

I tried to focus on Professor Frost's lecture about elemental balance in extreme weather conditions, but found my attention constantly drifting to that steady thread of connection that linked me to Fiona. Whatever she and Connor were discussing, it was important enough that her usual careful emotional control had given way to something more raw and honest.

Trust the partnership, I thought, remembering the advice Dr. Frost had given me weeks ago about allowing connections to develop naturally rather than trying to control every variable. *Let her process this in her own way, at her own pace.*

But as the lecture continued and I felt the conversation's emotional weight intensify, I found that easier said than done. Twenty years of training in political caution warred with the growing certainty that whatever decision Fiona reached would determine not just the future of our magical collaboration, but something far more personal.

When class ended, I felt her emotional state shift toward something that might have been determined hope. Before I could second-guess the impulse, I was walking toward wherever they were meeting, drawn by both concern for her well-being and the selfish need to know where we stood.

I found them sitting on a bench in the Winter Rose Garden, the same place where Fiona and I had shared our first moment of real vulnerability weeks ago. Snow fell gently around them, and Connor was speaking with the quiet authority that had made Santa trust him to lead the most important flight of the year despite being only a freshman.

"—strongest partnerships are the ones where both people choose to trust each other despite the risks involved," he was saying as I approached.

Both cousins looked up at my arrival. Connor's expression held the careful respect due to someone whose identity he probably suspected but was too diplomatic to voice. Fiona's eyes met mine, and through our bond, I felt her question about my emotional state, her willingness to give me whatever space I needed to process what came next.

"Connor," I said formally, inclining my head with genuine respect for his achievements. "I hope I'm not interrupting."

"Actually," Connor said, standing with a smile that carried surprising warmth, "I was just telling Fiona that the strongest partnerships are the ones where both people choose to trust each other despite the risks involved."

The words hit differently hearing them directly, especially coming from someone who'd successfully navigated high-stakes magical collaboration under extreme public pressure while maintaining his own challenging personal relationships.

Fiona stood to face me directly, and I felt the moment she reached some internal decision. "I've been thinking," she said. "About what you told me, about what it means, about what we're building together."

Through our bond, I braced myself for whatever conclusion she'd reached. Twenty years of political training had taught me to prepare for disappointment, for the moment when someone decided the risks of association with me outweighed any potential benefits.

"And?" I asked quietly, though I could sense my careful preparation for whatever decision she'd reached.

"And I think Connor's right about trusting the partnership," she said, reaching for my hands and immediately sending our magic into perfect harmony. "I think we're stronger together than either of us is individually, even when—especially when—things get complicated."

The relief that flooded through me was so intense that it probably overwhelmed our bond momentarily. But underneath it was something deeper: the recognition that she'd just chosen to face whatever came next as partners rather than trying to protect herself through distance.

For the first time in twenty years, someone had learned the full truth about my identity and chosen to stay rather than retreat to safer ground.

"Thank you," I said, and I meant it for both of them. Connor for providing the perspective that had helped her reach this decision, and Fiona for the trust that made it possible. "For the perspective, and for the trust."

"Thank you," Fiona said to Connor, "for reminding me that some things are worth the risk."

As we prepared to leave the garden, Connor caught Fiona's arm gently.

"One more thing," he said quietly, his voice carrying the wisdom of someone who'd learned to balance family legacy with personal identity under intense public scrutiny. "The family legacy pressure? It never really goes away, but it gets easier to carry when you have someone who understands the weight." He glanced at me, then back at Fiona. "And when you remember that you're not just living up to the name—you're making it your own."

His phone buzzed with what was probably another message from Kayla, and he smiled slightly. "Speaking of which, I should get back. Law school exam schedules wait for no one, even when you're trying to provide cousin wisdom across time zones."

Walking back toward the main campus with Fiona, our hands clasped and our magic flowing in perfect synchronization, I felt something I hadn't experienced since childhood: the certainty that I wasn't facing the future alone.

Whatever political challenges arose from my identity, whatever pressures the Frost Court brought to bear, whatever complications emerged from our magical partnership—we would handle them together.

For someone who'd spent two decades carefully managing every relationship to avoid exactly this kind of vulnerability, it should have been terrifying.

Instead, it felt like coming home.

CHAPTER SEVENTEEN
STORM WARNING

FIONA

I found Elian in the observatory, but he wasn't alone.

Professor Glacier stood near the crystalline windows, her massive frost giant form somehow managing to look elegant despite filling most of the circular room. When I entered, both she and Elian turned toward me with expressions that mixed relief with concern.

"Miss Prancer," Professor Glacier said, inclining her head formally. "How fortuitous. I was just explaining to Prince Elian the... developments that have occurred in your absence."

"Developments?" I looked between them, noting the tension in Elian's shoulders and the way frost patterns had spread across every surface in the room—a sure sign that his emotional control was strained.

"Magical instability," Elian said quietly, his pale eyes searching my face. "It started, not long after you..." He paused, clearly struggling with how to phrase it.

"After I started avoiding you," I finished, guilt twisting in my stomach. "What kind of instability?"

Professor Glacier gestured toward the windows, and I gasped at what I saw. The entire campus was covered in a thin layer of ice that pulsed with golden and silver light—our magical signatures, but chaotic and uncontrolled. Students moved carefully across the slippery pathways, and I could see maintenance crews working to clear ice from doorways and windows.

"It started small," the professor explained. "Frost forming in unusual patterns, minor temperature fluctuations. But it's been growing stronger throughout the day."

"Because our bond was severed," I realized, the implications hitting me like ice water. "The magical connection we've built—when I pulled away from it, it destabilized."

"Not severed," Elian corrected. "Strained. I could still feel you, but it was like..." He searched for the right words. "Like trying to hear music through static. The connection is there, but it's not flowing properly."

I moved closer to him, and immediately the chaotic frost patterns began to settle into more organized designs. The relief on his face was so obvious it made my chest ache.

"I'm sorry," I said quietly. "I let fear make my decisions instead of trusting what we've built together."

"What kind of fear?" he asked, though his tone suggested he already suspected.

I told him about the revelations regarding Deep Magic partnerships and their historical track record, about my terror that what we felt might not be real or that I might not be strong enough for what it could become. He already knew about Connor's speech.

"So you decided to test it," Elian said when I finished. "To see if our connection was genuine or just a magical influence."

"And?" Professor Glacier prompted, though her ancient eyes suggested she already knew the answer.

"And I felt like half of my soul was missing," I admitted. "Every instinct I have was screaming at me to find you, to fix whatever I'd broken. The magic wasn't driving me toward you—I was driving me toward you."

The frost patterns on the windows shifted into something beautiful and symmetrical as our bond settled back into harmony. But Professor Glacier's expression remained troubled.

"While your reunion is heartening," she said, "the magical instability you've triggered has caught the attention of parties beyond the university."

She moved to the center of the observatory and gestured with one massive hand. The air shimmered, and suddenly we were looking at a three-dimensional map of the surrounding region, dotted with pulsing lights that I realized represented magical monitoring stations.

"Each of these stations detected the fluctuations," she explained, pointing to clusters of rapidly blinking indicators. "The ripple effects extended nearly fifty miles in all directions."

My stomach dropped. "Fifty miles?"

"Deep Magic partnerships don't just affect the people involved," Professor Glacier said grimly. "They affect the entire magical ecosystem around them. When your bond destabilized, it created resonance cascades through every major magical nexus in the northern territories."

"What does that mean, practically?" Elian asked, though his pale complexion suggested he already suspected.

"It means," a new voice said from the observatory entrance, "that you've managed to get the attention of people who were perfectly content to ignore you before."

We turned to see Professor Blitzen entering, her silver hair crackling with more electrical energy than usual. Behind her came two figures I didn't recognize—a tall woman in midnight-blue robes and a shorter man whose very presence made the temperature in the room drop noticeably.

"Magistrate Stormwind," Professor Glacier said formally. "Lord Frostborn. I wasn't expecting you quite so soon."

Lord Frostborn. The name sent a chill through me that had nothing to do with temperature. I felt Elian go very still beside me, his hand finding mine instinctively.

"Uncle," Elian said quietly, and I heard volumes of complicated history in that single word.

"Prince Elian." The man inclined his head formally, but his ice-blue eyes—so similar to Elian's—carried no warmth. "Or should I say, Mr. Frost? I understand you've been operating under an assumed identity."

"The identity was provided for my protection," Elian replied carefully. "As you well know."

"Protection that has apparently failed spectacularly, given the magical disturbances you've created." Lord Frostborn's gaze shifted to me, and I felt like I was being evaluated by winter itself. "Miss Prancer, I presume. The catalyst for this... situation."

"I'm his partner," I said, lifting my chin despite the intimidation radiating from the man. "Academic and otherwise."

"Yes, so I've been told." His smile was as sharp as breaking ice. "How romantic. How completely inappropriate for someone of Prince Elian's station."

The casual dismissal stung, but before I could respond, Magistrate Stormwind stepped forward.

"Lord Frostborn, personal opinions aside, we're here to assess the situation objectively." She turned to Professor Blitzen. "What's the current status of their magical stability?"

"Restored, as of approximately twenty minutes ago," Professor

Blitzen replied. "The campus-wide anomalies ceased when they reestablished their bond."

"And their trial readiness?"

"Excellent, assuming no further disruptions." Professor Blitzen's tone carried a warning that didn't escape anyone in the room. "They've demonstrated remarkable progress in collaborative magic techniques."

"Progress that will be meaningless if they cannot maintain emotional stability," Lord Frostborn observed. "Today's incident proves that their partnership is fundamentally volatile."

"Today's incident," I said, my temper finally overriding my caution, "proves that our bond is real and necessary. When I tried to suppress it, the magic itself rebelled."

"An interesting theory," Magistrate Stormwind said thoughtfully. "And one that raises significant questions about the nature of your connection."

She gestured, and the air filled with swirling diagrams that looked like magical analysis charts. "The energy signatures we detected today match historical records of only three previous partnerships—all of which ended in either spectacular success or catastrophic failure."

"Which means?" Elian asked.

"Which means," Lord Frostborn said with evident satisfaction, "that your partnership represents exactly the kind of destabilizing force the courts have worked for centuries to prevent."

"Or," Professor Glacier interjected, "it represents exactly the kind of collaborative potential the courts have been too afraid to properly develop."

The temperature in the observatory dropped another ten degrees as Lord Frostborn's expression hardened. "The Frost Court has maintained stability for three centuries by avoiding precisely this kind of reckless experimentation."

"The same stability that led to my father's murder?" Elian asked quietly, and the words fell into the room like stones into still water.

"Careful, nephew." Lord Frostborn's voice carried a deadly warning. "Some subjects are not appropriate for public discussion."

"We're not in public," Elian replied, straightening to his full height. "We're in an academic setting, discussing the magical partnership I've chosen to pursue. My father's vision for collaborative magic is directly relevant to this conversation."

"Your father's vision nearly destroyed the realm."

"My father's vision was never given a proper chance to succeed." Elian's voice carried the authority he'd been born to wield, royal training finally overriding years of careful hiding. "It was suppressed by people who benefited from the current system of magical segregation."

The confrontation was escalating rapidly, and I could feel magical pressure building in the room as both men's powers responded to their emotional states. Ice was forming on every surface, and the aurora patterns visible through the windows were becoming agitated and chaotic.

"Enough," Magistrate Stormwind said firmly, and the authority in her voice made everyone take a step back. "Personal family dynamics aside, we're here to assess a specific situation."

She turned to face Elian and me directly. "The Frost Trials will proceed as scheduled in four days. However, given today's incident, the conditions have changed."

My heart sank. "Changed how?"

"You'll be performing under expanded oversight. Representatives from multiple courts, the Inter-Magical Stability Commission, and the Council of Seasonal Balance will be present to evaluate not just your academic progress, but your suitability for continued magical collaboration."

"In other words," Lord Frostborn added with evident satisfaction, "you'll be performing for the people who will decide whether your partnership is allowed to continue beyond these trials."

"And if we fail to meet their standards?" I asked, though I was pretty sure I didn't want to know the answer.

"Immediate separation and magical suppression," Magistrate Stormwind replied matter-of-factly. "For the safety of everyone involved."

The words hung in the air like a death sentence. Everything we'd built, everything we'd discovered about ourselves and each other, would be destroyed if we couldn't prove our worth to people who had already decided we were dangerous.

"However," Professor Blitzen said, stepping forward with characteristic defiance, "I should point out that several faculty members are prepared to testify on their behalf. Their progress has been exceptional by every measurable standard."

"Except emotional stability," Lord Frostborn observed. "Which today's incident proves is fundamentally lacking."

"Today's incident," I said, finding my voice again, "was caused by me making a fear-based decision to suppress our connection. It won't happen again."

"You seem very certain of that," Magistrate Stormwind said, though her tone suggested curiosity rather than skepticism.

"I am certain," I replied, reaching for Elian's hand. The moment our fingers touched, golden and silver light began to spiral around us, but this time it was controlled, purposeful, beautiful. "Because I understand now that our bond isn't something that can be turned on and off. It's fundamental to who we are when we're together."

"And if the pressure becomes too great?" Lord Frostborn pressed. "If the scrutiny, the expectations, the political implications prove overwhelming?"

I looked at Elian, seeing my own determination reflected in his pale eyes. "Then we'll face those challenges together, the way partnerships are supposed to work."

"Together," Elian agreed, his voice carrying absolute certainty.

The magical light around us intensified, and I felt our bond settling into a configuration that was deeper and more stable than anything we'd achieved before. The chaos from earlier in the day seemed like a distant memory compared to the harmony flowing between us now.

"Four days," Magistrate Stormwind said finally. "Use them wisely."

As the officials prepared to leave, Lord Frostborn paused at the observatory entrance.

"Prince Elian," he said quietly, "I hope you understand what you're risking. Not just for yourself, but for the future of the Frost Court itself."

"I understand that I'm building something worth risking everything for," Elian replied. "I think Father would have understood that too."

Lord Frostborn's expression flickered with something that might have been grief before the cold mask slipped back into place. "We shall see."

After they left, the observatory felt suddenly empty despite our presence. I moved to the windows, looking out at the campus that still sparkled with residual magical energy from our earlier disruption.

"Four days," I said softly.

"Four days," Elian agreed, joining me at the window. "Against opponents who've already decided we're too dangerous to succeed."

"Then we prove them wrong," I said, surprising myself with the confidence in my voice. "We show them that love and magic working together create something stronger than fear and control ever could."

Four days to save our future. Four days to prove that what we'd built was worth preserving.

Looking at Elian, feeling the absolute certainty of our connection humming beneath my skin, I thought we might actually have a chance.

If we could survive the pressure long enough to reach the trials at all.

CHAPTER EIGHTEEN

THE FROST TRIALS BEGIN

ELIAN

The morning of the trials dawned clear and cold, with an aurora that painted the sky in shades of silver and gold—colors that reminded me of the magical displays Fiona and I created together. Standing at my observatory window, I watched the formal carriages arrive on campus like pieces moving into position on a political chessboard.

Representatives from every major magical court in the northern hemisphere emerged in robes that declared their allegiances and intentions. The expanded oversight Magistrate Stormwind had promised was more extensive than even my court-trained political instincts had anticipated.

Through our bond, I could feel Fiona's mixture of terror and determination as she prepared in Shifter Lodge. Brynn's fox shifter energy provided warm support, offering hot chocolate and steady encouragement that made something tight in my chest ease slightly. At least Fiona had friends who would stand by her regardless of political complications.

The four days since the magical instability incident had been intensive for both of us—dawn-to-dusk training sessions with Professor Hoof, meditation work with Professor Glacier, and countless hours perfecting our synchronization until we could maintain perfect harmony even under deliberate stress. But more importantly, there had been days of rebuilding trust, of learning to be vulnerable with each other, of choosing partnership over the safety of emotional distance.

I dressed in my formal trial robes—silver-white with frost patterns that had been woven by master craftsmen in the Frost Court itself. The fabric carried subtle magical enhancements that would amplify my natural abilities, but I found myself thinking less about magical advantage and more about what these robes represented: the end of hiding, the acceptance of my true identity, the choice to stand as Prince Elian Frostborn rather than the anonymous transfer student I'd been pretending to be.

The Grand Arena had been transformed into something that resembled a formal court proceeding more than an academic evaluation. Crystalline viewing platforms rose in tiers around the central floor, while magical barriers hummed with protective energy designed to contain whatever power we might unleash.

But it was the audience that made my royal training kick into high alert.

The Frost Court delegation sat in formal arrangement, their midnight-blue robes creating a wall of austere authority that I recognized from childhood memories of state functions. Uncle Aldric—Lord Frostborn—occupied the center position, his expression carefully neutral as his pale eyes met mine across the arena. A slight nod, barely perceptible, acknowledged our family connection while maintaining appropriate political distance.

The other courts had positioned themselves with equal ceremony. Summer Court representatives blazed in golden robes that seemed to generate their own warmth, their magical signatures radiating the kind of confidence that came from believing they were the center of the magical world. Spring Court delegations wore living green that moved like wind-blown leaves, their power feeling fresh and optimistic despite the serious circumstances. The Autumn Court's burnt orange and deep red robes created an elegant contrast, their energy carrying the weight of harvests and endings, of cycles completing themselves.

And above them all, in a viewing box that seemed to float independently in the air, sat the three figures whose presence made every magical being in the arena instinctively straighten: the Council of Seasonal Balance, the highest magical authority in the realm.

This is it, I thought as Fiona appeared at my side. *No more pretending. No more hiding. Today we prove what collaborative magic can accomplish, or we fail publicly enough to justify every fear they've harbored about partnerships like ours.*

"Breathe," I said softly, though I wasn't sure if I was reassuring her or myself. She looked magnificent in her formal training robes—deep blue with silver threading that caught the light when she moved, colors that complemented my own robes in a way that had probably been planned by some thoughtful administrator. "They're here to judge our performance, not to execute us."

"The distinction feels academic," she replied, but I felt her steady herself through our bond, drawing on the same determination that had first attracted me to her months ago.

Through our connection, I could sense her awareness of the political weight pressing down on us from all sides. This wasn't just an academic trial—it was a public demonstration of whether magical partnerships between different species could handle the kind of pressure that royal alliances required.

Professor Hoof approached with her familiar mixture of pride and concern, offering final instructions that I barely heard over the sound of my own heartbeat. Professor Blitzen explained the trial phases with clinical precision: individual demonstration, collaborative construction, adaptive response. Each designed to test not just our magical abilities, but our fitness for the political responsibilities that would follow.

When Magistrate Stormwind's magically amplified voice called us to our positions, I felt the weight of hundreds of eyes studying our every movement. The monitoring equipment began to hum, recording magical signatures, emotional states, and compatibility readings that would be analyzed long after today was over.

Everything worthwhile is dangerous, I thought, remembering Master Wynne's words from so long ago. *And this partnership is definitely worthwhile.*

"Phase One," Magistrate Stormwind announced. "Individual demonstration. Each participant will display their magical abilities independently, without assistance from their partner."

The arena floor shifted, creating two separate platforms fifty feet apart. Close enough that I could still feel our bond like a warm constant in my chest, far enough that we would have to stand alone for the first time in weeks.

"Miss Prancer, you will demonstrate first."

Through our connection, I felt Fiona's spike of anxiety as she stepped onto her platform. The silence that fell over the arena was absolute, weighted with the expectations of people who were evaluating whether a middle-class reindeer shifter could stand as an equal partner to magical royalty.

Show them, I thought, pouring all my confidence through our bond. *Show them exactly who you are.*

When Fiona reached for her magic, I felt the moment she discovered how much the intensive training had changed her. The golden warmth that had always been beautiful became something deeper, more complex, connected to power that felt ancient and vast.

What she created took my breath away.

Light spiraled around her in patterns more intricate than anything I'd seen before, but this wasn't a mere magical display. She was telling the story of her people—reindeer in flight carrying hope to the furthest corners of the world, the courage required to bridge the gap between magical and mundane, the strength found in service to something larger than oneself.

Then she showed what she'd learned at NPU, and I felt tears sting my eyes as her magic reached toward my platform in acknowledgment of partnership even during individual demonstration. She understood, in a way that formal magical education had never taught me, that true power came through collaboration rather than domination.

When her magic finally settled, the silence stretched for heartbeats before applause erupted from every corner of the arena. Even representatives who had arrived determined to find fault were visibly moved by what they'd witnessed.

"Remarkable," someone whispered from the Council platform, and through our bond I felt Fiona's surge of pride and relief.

"Prince Elian," Magistrate Stormwind called. "Your demonstration."

My turn.

I stepped onto the platform and let twenty years of careful control finally drop away. Not the diplomatic restraint I'd maintained in public, but the deeper suppression of power that I'd learned was necessary for survival. For the first time since I was seven years old, I reached for the full scope of my magical inheritance.

The temperature in the arena plummeted as raw winter answered my call. But I wasn't just displaying power—I was creating art, architecture, beauty carved from the harshest element in nature. Ice erupted from my platform in crystalline spires that caught and reflected the aurora light streaming through the arena's dome, each structure singing with harmonic resonance that seemed to capture hope itself.

And woven through every frozen cathedral, every delicate spiral of ice, was a pattern that matched the rhythm of Fiona's heartbeat—visible proof that even in individual performance, I was thinking of our partnership, drawing strength from the connection we'd built together.

By the time I finished, the arena had been transformed into a winter wonderland so beautiful that several audience members were openly weeping. The ice structures seemed to hold light within them, creating an environment that was both magnificent and welcoming, powerful and protective.

That, I thought with satisfaction as the applause thundered around us, *is what royal ice magic looks like when it's powered by love instead of duty.*

"Phase Two," Magistrate Stormwind announced, and I felt our platforms merge back into a single space. "Collaborative construction. Participants will work together to create a magical structure that demonstrates both technical skill and artistic vision."

This was what we'd been training for—the chance to show what we could accomplish when our magic flowed together without reservation or fear. I moved to Fiona's side, and the moment our hands touched, I felt our individual demonstrations pale in comparison to what we could create together.

Golden warmth met crystalline precision in perfect harmony, but this was more than magical compatibility. This was emotional synchronization, intellectual partnership, spiritual union made manifest in ways that defied every textbook definition of collaborative magic.

What we built together transcended description.

It began as a bridge spanning the entire arena—ice and light woven together in patterns that seemed to dance and breathe with their own life. But it evolved into something far more complex: a living testament to what magical society could become if artificial barriers were dissolved in favor of genuine partnership.

Through our shared vision, I showed the court representatives scenes of collaboration that had never existed but could: partnerships between species that had been taught to fear each other, magical techniques that required multiple types of power to achieve their full potential, a future where diversity was celebrated as strength rather than tolerated as weakness.

The structure grew and changed, responding to both our conscious direction and the deeper truths that flowed through our bond. I felt Fiona's dreams of a world where magical ability mattered more than bloodline, where innovation was rewarded over tradition, where love was considered an asset rather than a liability in magical partnerships.

By the time we finished, the entire arena was filled with light and ice in perfect balance, creating an environment so beautiful and harmonious that the very air seemed to sing with possibility.

The applause was thunderous, but I was lost in the afterglow of our magic, in the absolute rightness of what we'd created together. Through our bond, I felt Fiona's matching awe and satisfaction—we had just proven beyond any doubt that collaborative magic wasn't just possible, but transformative.

"Phase Three," Magistrate Stormwind announced, and I felt my royal training snap into focus as our beautiful structure dissolved. "Adaptive response."

What appeared next made my blood turn to ice water.

The arena floor opened to reveal a chasm filled with chaotic magical energy—swirling darkness shot through with unstable power that set every protective instinct I'd inherited screaming warnings. This wasn't just a test of our magical abilities; this was a simulation of the kind of magical disaster that had historically destroyed entire kingdoms.

"A magical storm has trapped civilians," the magistrate explained. "You must work together to create a rescue pathway while containing the chaotic energy. Failure to maintain control will result in immediate trial termination."

Civilians. I looked into the chasm and saw them—magical constructs designed to simulate trapped individuals, but realistic enough that my conscience demanded action regardless of their artificial nature. This was the test that would determine whether our partnership could handle not just beauty and harmony, but crisis and life-or-death pressure.

"Together?" I asked Fiona, and heard the same fierce determination in her voice that I felt in my chest when she replied, "Together."

We stepped to the edge of the chasm, and I felt our bond deepen in ways I hadn't known were possible. The chaotic energy below us was designed to disrupt magical partnerships, to create exactly the kind of interference that forced collaborating mages apart when cooperation was most crucial.

But as we began to weave our magic together—my ice providing structure while her light provided guidance, my royal training offering strategic thinking while her shifter instincts found solutions that pure logic couldn't reach—I realized that everything we'd been through had prepared us for exactly this moment.

Not just the academic training, but the trust we'd built through honesty about our fears. The love we'd chosen despite political complications. The absolute certainty that whatever we faced, we would face it as partners rather than individuals trying to protect each other through separation.

The rescue was the most challenging magical working I'd ever attempted. Split-second timing was required to create pathways of stable magic through the chaotic storm, while perfect communication kept us synchronized despite the magical interference trying to tear our connection apart. But with each civilian construct we pulled to safety, we demonstrated something that no individual performance could have shown.

We proved that two people who trusted each other completely could accomplish the impossible.

As the arena returned to normal and the monitoring equipment powered down, I felt not exhaustion but exhilaration. We had shown them everything—individual mastery, collaborative beauty, crisis management, and the deep trust that made all of it possible.

"The trials are concluded," Magistrate Stormwind announced. "The evaluation committee will now deliberate. Results will be announced within the hour."

An hour to learn whether everything we'd built together would be allowed to continue, or whether political fear would override magical proof.

Looking at Fiona, seeing the pride and love and absolute certainty in her green eyes, I realized that regardless of the official verdict, we had already won the only battle that truly mattered.

We had proven to ourselves that our partnership was strong enough to handle anything the magical world could demand of it.

Everything worthwhile is dangerous, I thought, squeezing Fiona's hand as court representatives began their whispered consultations. *And this is definitely worthwhile.*

The rest was just politics.

CHAPTER NINETEEN
THE ROYAL EMISSARIES RETURN

FIONA

The hour of deliberation felt like an eternity.

Elian and I sat in a small preparation chamber adjacent to the arena, the magical residue from our trial's performance still humming beneath our skin. Through the crystalline walls, we could hear the muffled sounds of intense discussion from the evaluation committee—voices rising and falling in what was clearly a heated debate.

"They're arguing," I observed, pressing my ear closer to the wall.

"Extensively," Elian agreed, his expression troubled. "I can make out Lord Frostborn's voice, and he doesn't sound pleased."

Before I could respond, the chamber door burst open. But instead of Professor Hoof or one of the other faculty members we'd been expecting, three figures in formal court regalia entered —their midnight-blue robes so dark they seemed to absorb light from the room.

"Prince Elian," the center figure said, pulling back his hood to reveal sharp features and eyes like chips of winter sky. "By order of the Frost Court Council, you are commanded to return home immediately."

My blood turned to ice. These weren't observers or evaluators —these were court enforcers, the kind of officials who didn't take no for an answer.

"Chancellor Arcturus," Elian said quietly, rising to his feet with the fluid grace that marked his royal breeding. "I wasn't expecting a personal visit."

"Weren't you?" The Chancellor's smile was sharp. "Surely you realized that today's... exhibition would attract official attention. The magical displays you've been creating, the publicity surrounding your partnership—did you think the court would ignore such developments indefinitely?"

"I thought the court understood that I was completing my education as agreed," Elian replied carefully. "The trials are part of that educational process."

"The trials are a sideshow," one of the other enforcers said dismissively. "A distraction from your real responsibilities. The Frost Court has need of its heir."

"What kind of need?" I asked, though something about the way they were avoiding eye contact with me suggested I wasn't really part of this conversation.

Chancellor Arcturus glanced at me with barely concealed irritation. "Miss Prancer, while your... association with Prince Elian has been noted, matters of court business are not your concern."

"Anything that affects my partner is my concern," I replied, standing to move beside Elian. The moment I did, I felt our magical bond flare protectively, golden light beginning to spiral around my hands.

"Partner." The Chancellor said the word like it tasted unpleas-

ant. "Yes, we've heard about this alleged partnership. Most irregu-
lar. Most inappropriate for someone of the Prince's station."

"There's nothing inappropriate about it," Elian said, his voice
carrying the authority he'd been born to wield. "My partnership
with Fiona has been officially recognized by the university and
evaluated by multiple magical authorities."

"Academic partnerships," the third enforcer said with obvious
disdain, "are not the same as the binding alliances required of
royal heirs. The court has identified several suitable candidates
for your eventual marriage—all from appropriate bloodlines, all
capable of strengthening our political position."

Marriage candidates. The words hit me like ice water. Of
course. I'd been so focused on the trials, on proving our magical
compatibility, that I'd somehow forgotten the most basic political
reality: princes didn't get to choose their own partners.

"I've already chosen my partner," Elian said firmly, his hand
finding mine. "And my choice isn't subject to court approval."

Chancellor Arcturus laughed, the sound sharp and cold. "Your
choice? Prince Elian, you seem to have developed some very
romantic notions about royal prerogatives. The Frost Court has
survived for millennia precisely because personal desires are
subordinated to political necessity."

"The way my father's desires were subordinated?" Elian asked
quietly, and the temperature in the room dropped noticeably.

"Your father," the Chancellor replied with deadly calm,
"nearly destroyed the realm with his experiments in collaborative
magic. We will not allow his son to repeat those mistakes."

"Collaborative magic like what we demonstrated today?" I
interjected, my temper finally overriding caution. "Magic that
saved lives, created beauty, proved that different types of power
working together are stronger than any individual ability?"

"Magic that destabilized an entire region," the first enforcer countered. "Magic that requires constant monitoring to prevent catastrophic overflow. Magic that proves Miss Prancer is either unwilling or unable to control forces beyond her comprehension."

The accusation stung because it contained a grain of truth. The magical instability from four days ago had affected a fifty-mile radius, and while it had been resolved quickly, the implications were undeniable.

"The instability was temporary," Elian said. "A learning experience that led to better control, not evidence of fundamental incompatibility."

"Was it?" Chancellor Arcturus gestured, and the air filled with swirling charts that looked like magical analysis reports. "Because our intelligence suggests otherwise. Reports of uncontrolled manifestations, of emotional volatility affecting magical output, of a partnership that operates more on feeling than rational control."

Looking at the data—cold, clinical, stripped of all context—I could see how our partnership might appear dangerous to people who valued stability above all else.

"Prince Elian," the Chancellor continued, "you will return to the court for proper evaluation of your magical abilities and discussion of your future role. This partnership experiment has gone far enough."

"And if I refuse?" Elian asked.

"Refusal is not an option." The second enforcer stepped forward, and I could see magical restraints beginning to form around his hands. "You are the heir to the Frost Court. Your personal preferences are irrelevant compared to your duty to the realm."

The magical restraints reached toward Elian, but before they could make contact, golden light erupted from my hands with enough force to shatter them entirely. The room filled with the harmonic resonance of our bond as my magic rose to protect what mattered most to me.

"Don't," I said quietly, power crackling around me like visible anger. "Don't you dare treat him like property to be retrieved."

"Miss Prancer," Chancellor Arcturus said, his voice carrying new respect alongside the warning, "you are interfering with official court business. Stand down, or face the consequences."

"What consequences?" I asked, taking a step forward. "You're going to arrest me for defending my partner? You're going to declare war on North Pole University for protecting its students?"

"If necessary," the Chancellor replied coldly.

Before the confrontation could escalate further, the chamber door opened again. This time, it was Magistrate Stormwind, flanked by two other Council of Seasonal Balance members I recognized from the viewing box.

"Chancellor Arcturus," she said pleasantly, though her tone carried unmistakable authority. "How unexpected to find you here. I wasn't aware the Frost Court had jurisdiction over students taking their trials."

"The trials are concluded," the Chancellor replied. "Prince Elian's academic obligations have been fulfilled. He is now required to return home."

"Actually," Magistrate Stormwind said with a smile that didn't reach her eyes, "the trials have reached the deliberation phase. Until a final decision is rendered, all participants remain under Council protection."

The legal technicality hung in the air like a shield. I could see the Chancellor calculating whether he wanted to challenge the Council of Seasonal Balance directly.

"Furthermore," another Council member added, "any attempt

to remove participants before the conclusion of official proceedings would constitute interference with inter-court judicial processes. I'm sure the Frost Court wouldn't want to create a diplomatic incident over a student evaluation."

Chancellor Arcturus's expression went through several interesting changes before settling on barely controlled fury. "This is a temporary delay, nothing more. Prince Elian's obligations to the court supersede any academic commitments."

"Perhaps," Magistrate Stormwind replied diplomatically. "But those obligations will have to wait until our proceedings are complete."

The standoff stretched for several tense moments. I could feel Elian's magic coiled and ready beside mine, prepared for whatever might come next. But after what felt like hours, Chancellor Arcturus stepped back.

"Very well," he said coldly. "We will await the Council's decision. But Prince Elian, understand that this reprieve is temporary. The court's patience is not infinite."

"Neither is mine," Elian replied quietly, and there was something in his voice that made all three enforcers look at him with new attention.

After they left, the chamber felt suddenly empty despite our presence and that of the Council members.

"Thank you," I said to Magistrate Stormwind. "Though I suspect that was more about legal procedure than personal protection."

"You'd be surprised," she replied with a genuine smile. "The Council has been watching your partnership with great interest. Your performance today was... illuminating."

"In what way?" Elian asked.

"In every way that matters for the decision we're about to

render." She moved toward the door, then paused. "One piece of advice: whatever we decide today, the political pressure you're facing is only going to intensify. Make sure you're prepared for that reality."

After the Council members left, Elian and I stood alone in the chamber, the weight of everything that had just happened settling around us like a heavy cloak.

"They're going to try to separate us," I said quietly. "One way or another, they're going to find a way to end this partnership."

"Let them try," Elian replied, his voice carrying the steel that twenty years of hiding had forged in him. "I've spent my entire life being told what I owe to other people's expectations. I'm done with that."

"But the court, your responsibilities, your father's legacy—"

"My father's legacy," he interrupted, "was believing that love and collaboration could change the world for the better. Honoring that legacy means choosing to fight for what we've built together, not surrendering to people who killed him for having similar ideas."

Looking at him—seeing not a reluctant prince but someone who had finally found his true purpose—I felt a surge of fierce pride. Whatever political storms were coming, whatever forces aligned against us, we would face them together.

"Some things are worth any fight," I said, the conviction in my voice surprising me.

"And this," he replied, pulling me closer as our magic flared around us in defiant harmony, "is definitely worth fighting for."

Through the crystalline walls, we could hear the debate in the evaluation chamber reaching a crescendo. In moments, we would learn whether our partnership had a future.

But looking at Elian, feeling the absolute certainty of our bond despite every attempt to break it, I realized that the trials had already given us something more valuable than official approval.

They had proven that what we felt for each other was stronger than duty, politics, or fear.

Now we just had to prove it was strong enough to survive what came next.

CHAPTER TWENTY

POWER UNLEASHED

ELIAN

The deliberation stretched on for another hour, each minute feeling like an eternity as voices rose and fell behind the chamber walls. My enhanced hearing, trained through years of court intrigue, caught fragments of heated argument that made my royal instincts snap to attention.

"They're deadlocked," I told Fiona quietly, pressing my ear to the crystalline wall. "I can hear Uncle Aldric arguing with someone from the Summer Court, and it's getting heated."

The political implications were staggering. A deadlocked evaluation committee meant that our partnership had divided the magical establishment so fundamentally that they couldn't reach consensus. In court politics, that usually led to one of two outcomes: compromise that satisfied no one, or escalation that satisfied everyone's worst fears.

Through our bond, I could feel Fiona's anxiety mixing with determination. Whatever the verdict, we had proven something crucial to ourselves today—that our partnership could handle pressure, crisis, and impossible challenges without breaking apart.

When Professor Blitzen appeared with her barely contained electrical energy crackling around her silver hair, I knew the waiting was over. Her careful composure couldn't quite hide the tension that suggested the committee's decision would be complicated rather than simple.

"The evaluation committee has reached a decision," she said. "They're ready to announce the results."

As we walked back toward the arena, I found myself drawing on twenty years of royal training in maintaining composure under pressure. Whatever came next—acceptance, rejection, conditional approval, or something unprecedented—I would face it as Prince Elian Frostborn rather than the hidden student I'd been pretending to be.

The reconfigured arena resembled a formal court proceeding, with audience members arranged in a semicircle and the evaluation committee positioned on a raised platform that emphasized their authority. Magistrate Stormwind stood behind her crystal podium like a judge preparing to render a verdict on more than just academic performance.

"Participants Fiona Prancer and Elian Frost," she announced, and I noted the deliberate use of my assumed name rather than my royal title. "Please take your positions."

Walking to the center of the arena floor, I felt the weight of hundreds of eyes studying our every movement with renewed intensity. But instead of the intimidation I might have expected, I felt something closer to peace. We had demonstrated our truth as completely as possible. The rest was politics.

"The evaluation committee has reviewed your performance in all three phases of the Frost Trials," Magistrate Stormwind continued, her formal tone suggesting carefully negotiated language. "Your individual demonstrations showed exceptional skill and artistic vision. Your collaborative construction exceeded all expectations for technical complexity and emotional resonance."

Through our bond, I felt Fiona's guarded optimism. But my court-trained instincts recognized the pause that followed as the moment when positive assessment would be balanced against concerning observations.

"However," she continued, and I braced for political calculation disguised as academic evaluation, "the adaptive response phase raised concerns about the stability of your magical bond under extreme stress."

Of course. They would focus on the moment when we'd pushed beyond safe parameters to save lives, rather than on our success in maintaining control despite chaotic interference.

"The magical readings during the rescue scenario showed power fluctuations that exceeded safe parameters," Magistrate Stormwind explained with clinical precision. "At several points, your combined energy output approached levels that could have caused structural damage to the arena itself."

"But we maintained control," Fiona said, unable to keep quiet despite the formal setting. Through our bond, I felt her frustration at having our greatest success reframed as evidence of danger. "We completed the rescue, contained the chaotic energy, and protected everyone involved."

"You did," the magistrate agreed with diplomatic acknowledgment. "But the question before this committee is not whether you can succeed under optimal conditions. The question is whether your partnership represents a safe and stable magical development, or a potential threat that requires ongoing oversight."

Ongoing oversight. The phrase sent ice through my veins

because I recognized it from court documents I'd studied during my political education. It meant conditional acceptance designed to maintain control rather than genuine approval.

Before I could process the implications fully, chaos erupted in the audience section.

"This is exactly the kind of power-hungry collaboration that destroyed the old kingdoms!"

The voice came from the Frost Court delegation—not Uncle Aldric, but one of the younger representatives whose hostility reminded me uncomfortably of Chancellor Arcturus's faction. Through our bond, I felt Fiona's hurt at the accusation, her confusion about why success was being treated as evidence of dangerous ambition.

"Destroyed them, or transformed them into something better?" Professor Glacier shot back with the kind of authority that came from centuries of accumulated wisdom. "Because the historical record is far from clear on that point."

"The historical record," Uncle Aldric said, rising with the cold authority that had made him an effective court leader, "shows that Deep Magic partnerships inevitably destabilize the careful balance that maintains peace between the courts."

I wanted to argue, to point out that the historical record had been written by people who benefited from suppressing collaborative magic. But before I could speak, Professor Blitzen stepped forward with her characteristic defiance of political pressure.

"The historical record was written by the victors," she declared. "By people who benefited from the suppression of collaborative magic."

The argument escalated rapidly, with representatives taking sides based on centuries-old political alliances rather than what they'd actually witnessed today. Through my enhanced senses, I could feel magical pressure building in the room as emotions ran high and careful control began to slip.

That's when I realized we had a much bigger problem than political disagreement.

A young Spring Court representative suddenly stood up, his face pale with genuine terror. "Can't you feel it?" he asked, his voice cracking with strain. "The resonance—it's getting stronger. Their bond is affecting everyone in the room."

Oh, hell. He was right. The magical signature that Fiona and I generated together had been expanding unconsciously, reaching out to touch every magical being in the arena. Instead of remaining neutral, it was amplifying whatever emotions people were already feeling—confidence in our supporters, fear in our opponents.

"Fiona," I said quietly, my royal crisis management training kicking in, "we need to contain this. Now."

Through our bond, I felt her reach for our connection to try to pull back the expanding resonance. But instead of contracting, our magic surged outward with even greater force, seeking minds and hearts that could understand what we were trying to build.

This is exactly what they've been afraid of, I realized with growing horror. *Uncontrolled magical influence that grows beyond our ability to manage it.*

The young Spring Court representative gasped and sat down hard, his eyes going wide with wonder. "I can feel what they feel," he whispered. "The connection, the harmony—it's beautiful."

"It's dangerous," Uncle Aldric snapped, though I could hear the uncertainty beneath his conviction. Even he was being affected by our expanding resonance, and I watched him struggle to maintain opposition in the face of emotions that were becoming impossible to ignore.

"Stop this," Chancellor Arcturus commanded from his position in the audience. "You're proving exactly why this partnership cannot be allowed to continue. Uncontrolled magical influence over unwilling participants—"

"We're not unwilling," Marcus interrupted, and I felt a surge of gratitude for his courage in standing up despite the political pressure. "We can choose whether to accept the connection or reject it. And I choose to accept it."

More voices joined his—Brynn, other students from our network, faculty members who had been touched by our magic during training sessions. One by one, they were declaring their willingness to be part of something larger than traditional magical isolation.

But I could also see the opposition: older court representatives actively fighting against our expanding resonance, their magical defenses flaring as they tried to block our influence.

"This is exactly what we feared," Uncle Aldric said with new urgency. "A magical influence that grows beyond the ability of its originators to control."

He was right, and that terrified me more than any court intrigue ever had. What had started as an attempt to contain our expanding magic had become a demonstration of exactly why some people considered our partnership an existential threat to magical society.

"Fiona, Elian," Magistrate Stormwind called out, her voice sharp with authority, "you must contain this resonance immediately, or we will be forced to implement emergency suppression protocols."

Emergency suppression. I knew what that meant—magical barriers designed to sever our connection entirely, regardless of the consequences to either of us. The kind of intervention that had historically left both partners magically crippled.

"Together," I said to Fiona, reaching for her hand with

desperate hope that our combined will could pull back what we'd unconsciously unleashed. "We pull it back together."

But the moment our hands touched, instead of containing the expanding resonance, we triggered something far more dramatic.

The magical network that had been growing unconsciously suddenly snapped into perfect clarity. Every person in the arena who had been touched by our connection found themselves linked not just to us, but to each other. Political opponents could suddenly sense each other's genuine motivations. Supporters and skeptics alike experienced perspectives they'd never considered.

For one perfect, terrifying moment, the arena became a living example of what magical society could become if collaboration replaced competition, if understanding replaced fear.

This is what Father envisioned, I thought with sudden, startling clarity. *Not just partnerships between individuals, but networks of connection that made empathy inevitable.*

And then reality crashed back down.

"Enough!"

The voice boomed through the arena with enough force to make the crystalline walls ring like bells. One of the Council of Seasonal Balance members I hadn't seen before stood in the floating observation box, power radiating from her in waves that made my royal magical training recognize absolute authority when I encountered it.

With a gesture that looked deceptively casual, she severed every connection in the expanding network except the core bond between Fiona and me.

The sudden silence was deafening. I felt dozens of people struggling to catch their breath after the intensity of shared connection, their faces mixing wonder with relief at being returned to the familiar isolation of their individual perspectives.

"Participants Prancer and Frost," the Council member said,

her voice carrying the kind of absolute authority that made even Uncle Aldric straighten reflexively, "you have just demonstrated both the potential and the danger of your partnership in the most dramatic way possible."

Through our bond, I felt Fiona's mixture of pride and terror at what we'd accomplished. We had proven that collaborative magic could create genuine understanding between opposing factions—but we'd also proven that such magic operated beyond normal control parameters.

"However," the Council member continued, "you have also demonstrated something that the evaluation committee did not expect to see—the ability to create genuine collaborative networks that respect individual choice while fostering under-standing between disparate groups."

She gestured to the audience, where I could see people looking at each other with new expressions. Not necessarily agreement, but comprehension. The brief moment of shared experience had given everyone insight into perspectives they'd never considered before.

"The Council of Seasonal Balance renders the following deci-sion," she announced with formal ceremony. "The partnership between Fiona Prancer and Elian Frost has successfully completed the Frost Trials and demonstrated exceptional collaborative potential."

Relief flooded through our bond so intensely that I nearly staggered. We had won. Against all political odds, despite demon-strating exactly the kind of uncontrolled power that terrified magical authorities, we had been accepted.

"But," she continued, and I braced for the conditions that would inevitably follow, "given the unprecedented nature of their magical development, they will continue their studies under expanded oversight and with mandatory training in large-scale magical containment."

Through our bond, I felt Fiona's question about practical implications, but I already understood what "expanded oversight" meant in political terms. We would be valuable assets now, too important to suppress but too powerful to ignore. Our every magical development would be studied, our techniques would be analyzed, and our future choices would carry implications far beyond personal preference.

"It means," Magistrate Stormwind said with a smile that mixed congratulation with warning, "that you've proven your partnership is too valuable to suppress and too powerful to ignore. Congratulations. You've just become the most closely watched students in the history of magical education."

As the arena began to empty and court delegations prepared to return to their respective territories, I felt the weight of what we'd achieved settling around me like a royal mantle. We had won more than just academic acceptance—we had forced the magical establishment to acknowledge that collaborative magic could create understanding rather than just power.

But we had also revealed capabilities that would make us valuable to some people and threatening to others. The political storm that had been building around us was about to become a hurricane of competing interests.

"Ready for what comes next?" I asked Fiona, my hand still linked with hers as our magic settled into stable patterns that would probably be monitored and analyzed for years to come.

"With you as my partner?" she replied, echoing our old call-and-response with new meaning now that we'd officially become a force that could reshape magical society. "I think we can handle anything."

Looking around the arena at faces that had been briefly

connected to our vision of collaborative magic, I felt not fear but anticipation. We hadn't just passed the trials—we had planted seeds of change that could grow into something revolutionary.

The real trials were just beginning. But now we faced them not as students trying to prove ourselves, but as partners who had demonstrated we could handle anything the magical world demanded of us.

CHAPTER TWENTY-ONE

THE CLAIM

FIONA

The hours after the trials passed in a blur of congratulations, formal paperwork, and the kind of political maneuvering that made my head spin. Representatives from various courts approached us with offers of "enhanced training opportunities" that sounded suspiciously like recruitment attempts, while university officials worked frantically to establish the new oversight protocols the Council had mandated.

But through it all, I was acutely aware of Chancellor Arcturus watching from the edges of every conversation, his expression promising that the Frost Court's business with Elian was far from concluded.

"We need to talk," Professor Blitzen said quietly, appearing at my elbow as yet another court representative finished explaining why their "collaborative magic research program" would be perfect for someone of my talents. "Both of you. My office, ten minutes."

The tone in her voice suggested this wasn't a request.

We found her office already occupied when we arrived. Lord Frostborn sat in one of the chairs facing her desk, his formal robes making him look like a piece of living winter. Beside him, Chancellor Arcturus studied a stack of documents that made my stomach clench with foreboding.

"Sit," Professor Blitzen said, gesturing to the remaining chairs. "We have decisions to make, and not much time to make them."

"What kind of decisions?" I asked, though the grim expressions around the room suggested I didn't want to know.

"The kind that will determine whether your partnership survives the next twenty-four hours," Lord Frostborn replied bluntly. "The trials may be over, but the political implications are just beginning."

Chancellor Arcturus looked up from his documents, his pale eyes calculating. "Prince Elian, the Frost Court Council has reviewed today's proceedings and reached a conclusion. Your magical development has progressed beyond what can be safely managed through remote oversight."

"Meaning?" Elian asked, though his tone suggested he already suspected.

"Meaning that our earlier conversation about you returning to the court immediately for intensive training in royal magical protocols is no longer a conversation but reality," the Chancellor replied. "Your partnership with Miss Prancer, while academically successful, represents a political liability that can no longer be ignored."

"No," I said, the word coming out harder than I'd intended. "He's not going."

Chancellor Arcturus turned his attention to me, and I felt like I was being evaluated by winter itself. "Miss Prancer, while your emotional attachment is understandable, Prince Elian's obligations extend far beyond personal preference. He is the heir to a magical throne. His first duty is to the realm, not to academic partnerships."

"His first duty," I shot back, "is to be true to himself and the magic that chose us both. You saw what we accomplished today. You felt the network we created, the connections we fostered between people who had never understood each other before."

"I felt magical influence being exerted over unwilling participants," the Chancellor replied coldly. "I felt the kind of uncontrolled power expansion that historically leads to catastrophic magical wars."

"You felt collaboration," Professor Blitzen interjected firmly. "You felt what happens when artificial barriers between magical types are dissolved in favor of genuine understanding."

"I felt chaos," Lord Frostborn said quietly, but there was something in his expression that suggested the experience had affected him more than he wanted to admit. "However... I also felt something I had not expected."

He paused, studying Elian with what might have been pride alongside the concern.

"I felt the emergence of true royal magic," he continued. "Not just power, but the kind of leadership ability that could indeed transform our magical society. The question is whether such transformation would be beneficial or catastrophic."

"There's only one way to find out," Elian said, straightening in his chair with the authority he'd been born to wield. "And that's to let us continue developing this partnership under proper guidance, not to separate us out of fear."

"Prince Elian," Chancellor Arcturus said with barely concealed frustration, "you seem to believe you have a choice in this matter. Allow me to clarify: you do not. The Frost Court has legal authority over its heir, regardless of his personal preferences."

"Does it?" Professor Blitzen asked mildly, producing a document that glowed with official seals. "Because, according to the Council of Seasonal Balance's ruling, both participants in today's trials are now under inter-court protection pending the establishment of their new training protocols."

The Chancellor's expression went thunderous. "A temporary legal technicality—"

"A binding magical contract," Professor Blitzen corrected. "One that supersedes individual court authority when it comes to students who have demonstrated capabilities that affect inter-court relations."

She handed the document to Lord Frostborn, who read it with an expression that grew increasingly troubled.

"This grants them protected status for the remainder of the academic year," he said finally. "But it also requires them to submit to oversight from all four seasonal courts, not just the Frost Court."

"Which means?" I asked.

"Which means," Chancellor Arcturus said with obvious displeasure, "that your partnership has become a matter of inter-court politics rather than internal Frost Court business."

The implications hit me like ice water. We weren't just dealing with one court's disapproval anymore—we were now subjects of interest to the entire magical political establishment.

"However," Lord Frostborn continued, "there are... opportunities in this development. Prince Elian, if you are determined to pursue this path despite court opposition, you will need to do so with full commitment and understanding of the consequences."

"What kind of consequences?" Elian asked.

"The kind that requires you to claim your birthright publicly rather than hiding behind assumed identities," his uncle replied. "If you're going to challenge centuries of magical tradition, you must do so as Prince Elian Frostborn, not as a university student playing at anonymity."

The weight of that statement settled over the room like a heavy blanket. Because claiming his birthright publicly meant accepting all the responsibilities and dangers that came with being the lost heir to the Frost Court.

"And Miss Prancer," Lord Frostborn continued, turning his attention to me, "if you are determined to bind yourself to the Frost Court's heir, you must understand that you are no longer simply a student or even simply a magical partner. You are a political figure whose actions will affect the stability of the realm."

I felt Elian's hand find mine under the table, our bond humming with shared determination.

"I understand," I said quietly.

"Do you?" Chancellor Arcturus leaned forward. "Do you understand that royal partnerships are not just romantic attachments, but political alliances that affect trade agreements, territorial boundaries, and the balance of power between courts? Do you understand that choosing to claim Prince Elian as your partner means accepting responsibility for the welfare of millions of magical beings?"

The scope of what he was describing made my head spin, but underneath the intimidation was something else—a challenge. They were offering us the chance to be not just partners, but leaders. Not just collaborators, but revolutionaries.

"Then we claim each other," I said, surprising myself with the steadiness of my voice. "Publicly, completely, with full understanding of what it means."

"Fiona," Elian said quietly, "you don't have to—"

"Yes, I do," I interrupted, turning to face him fully. "Because you were right—hiding behind assumed identities and academic pretenses isn't working anymore. If we're going to prove that collaborative magic can change the world, we need to do it as ourselves. Completely and honestly."

I stood up, drawing courage from the certainty I felt through our bond.

"Prince Elian Frostborn," I said formally, "I claim you as my magical partner, my equal, my chosen companion for whatever comes next. Not because of your title or your power, but because of who you are when we're together."

The words carried more weight than I'd expected. The moment I spoke them, I felt something shift in the magical atmosphere of the room—a sense of completion, of destiny finally acknowledged.

Elian rose to face me, his pale eyes blazing with determination and love.

"Fiona Prancer," he replied, his voice carrying the authority of centuries of royal tradition, "I claim you as my partner, my equal, my chosen companion. Not because it's politically convenient or magically advantageous, but because loving you has made me into the person I was meant to become."

Golden and silver light erupted around us, but this time it felt different—not chaotic or overwhelming, but ceremonial. Purposeful. Like the magic itself was acknowledging what we'd declared.

"Well," Professor Blitzen said with obvious satisfaction, "that's legally binding under both university regulations and inter-court magical law."

Chancellor Arcturus looked like he'd swallowed something particularly unpleasant. "This changes nothing. Prince Elian still has obligations to the court that supersede personal attachments."

"Actually," Lord Frostborn said quietly, "it changes every-thing. A formal claiming between magical partners of this caliber

creates bonds that cannot be severed without catastrophic consequences to both parties."

He stood, moving to the window that overlooked the campus.
"Furthermore, a royal claiming that is witnessed and acknowledged by representatives of multiple courts creates new political
realities that must be accommodated rather than opposed."

"You're saying they've maneuvered us into accepting their
partnership?" the Chancellor asked with obvious displeasure.

"I'm saying they've maneuvered themselves into a position
where their partnership becomes a cornerstone of inter-court
relations rather than a threat to them," Lord Frostborn replied.
"Quite clever, actually. Very much what I would have expected
from Boreas's son."

The mention of Elian's father hung in the air like a benedic-
tion, and I saw something shift in Lord Frostborn's expression—
not approval exactly, but recognition.

"So what happens now?" I asked.

"Now," Professor Blitzen said with a grin, "you finish your
education under the most intensive magical oversight in history.
And you prove that what you've claimed today was worth the
revolution it's about to cause."

As we prepared to leave the office, Lord Frostborn caught
Elian's arm gently.

"Your father would be proud," he said quietly. "Though I
suspect he would also be terrified by the path you've chosen."

"Good," Elian replied. "Everything worthwhile is dangerous."

"Indeed it is," his uncle agreed.

Walking back across campus hand in hand, our claiming still
resonating through our bond like music, I felt a deep sense of
completion. We weren't hiding anymore. We weren't pretending
to be something we weren't.

We were exactly what we'd been meant to be from the beginning—partners, equals, and the beginning of something that could change the magical world forever.

The question was whether that world was ready for what we represented.

Looking at Elian, feeling the absolute certainty of our bond humming beneath my skin, I thought we might just be strong enough to find out.

CHAPTER TWENTY-TWO
A NEW BEGINNING

ELIAN

The news of our public claiming spread across campus faster than wildfire, but I was too focused on the shift in Fiona's magical signature to pay attention to the whispered conversations that followed in our wake. Through our bond, I could feel her processing the magnitude of what we'd done—not just the political implications, but the personal transformation from academic partners to something unprecedented in magical society.

By the time we reached Shifter Lodge, crowds had already gathered in the common room. The moment we entered, conversation stopped abruptly, and I found myself under the kind of scrutiny I hadn't experienced since my last formal court function at age seven.

But this was different. These weren't court officials calculating my political value—these were Fiona's friends, trying to understand how her life had just changed and what it might mean for their connection to her.

"Well," Brynn said with characteristic directness, "that's one way to make things official."

A nervous laugh rippled through the crowd, but the tension didn't ease. Through my enhanced senses, I could feel their curiosity pressing against Fiona like a physical weight—questions about royal partnerships, speculation about our future, wonder about whether she would still be accessible to them now that formal protocol surrounded our relationship.

They're afraid they're losing her, I realized, watching their faces. *The same way court officials used to look at my father when he spent time with common-born advisors.*

"Can we talk?" Fiona asked Brynn quietly, and I caught the strain in her voice that came from trying to process too much change too quickly. "Somewhere private?"

I watched them head upstairs, followed by Marcus, and felt a familiar pang of isolation. Not rejection—Fiona needed space to work through this with people who'd known her before royal complications entered her life. But the reminder that there were parts of her experience I couldn't share, friendships that predated our partnership and would require careful navigation now that political protocol affected every interaction.

While they talked, I retreated to a quiet corner of the common room and tried to process my own transformation. For twenty years, I'd hidden my identity so completely that sometimes I'd almost forgotten who I was beneath the careful anonymity. Now, in the span of a single afternoon, I'd reclaimed my name, my title, and my birthright.

Prince Elian Frostborn. The name felt both foreign and familiar, like putting on clothes that had been carefully stored away and finding they still fit despite years of growth.

Through our bond, I could sense the conversation happening upstairs—Marcus's wonder at royal complications, Brynn's concern about changing dynamics, Fiona's struggle to understand how she could remain herself while accepting unprecedented responsibility.

"Princess," I felt her shock at the word, her realization that claiming me meant accepting not just my love but my entire political inheritance. The thought made something twist in my stomach because I knew exactly how overwhelming that transition could be.

When Professor Hoof's presence approached through the lodge's corridors, I felt the shift from personal processing to official business. Her magical signature carried the weight of administrative urgency that suggested our claiming had triggered immediate practical complications.

Twenty minutes later, I found myself in the university's formal conference room, surrounded by the kind of high-level political meeting I'd been trained for since childhood but had hoped never to experience again. Uncle Aldric sat at the head of the table with the natural authority that made him an effective court leader. Chancellor Arcturus occupied the position of primary advisor, though his expression suggested he'd rather be anywhere else. Professor Blitzen and the university dean provided an academic perspective, while Magistrate Stormwind's magical projection added inter-court authority to the proceedings.

Fiona sat beside me, and through our bond, I could feel her complete disorientation at finding herself in the middle of magical politics at the highest level. Twenty years of court training had prepared me for exactly this kind of meeting, but she was navigating it through pure instinct and determination.

"Miss Prancer," Uncle Aldric began without preamble, "your claiming of Prince Elian has created certain... complications that must be addressed immediately."

Complications. The diplomatic language made me wince

because I knew exactly what those complications involved. Succession law hadn't anticipated the heir to a major court forming a permanent magical bond outside established nobility. Trade agreements would need renegotiation. Territorial boundaries might shift. Inter-court relationships that had been stable for centuries would require careful rebalancing.

"The kind that arise when the heir to a major court forms a permanent magical bond with someone outside the established nobility," Chancellor Arcturus replied to Fiona's question with barely concealed disapproval. "Succession law, territorial agreements, trade negotiations—your partnership affects all of it."

Through our bond, I felt Fiona's growing understanding of just how much her life had changed in the space of a few formal words. She hadn't just claimed a romantic partner—she'd become a central figure in magical politics, whether she wanted to or not.

"Furthermore," Magistrate Stormwind added, her projected presence flickering slightly with the magical energy required to maintain long-distance communication, "your demonstrated ability to create magical networks that span different species and courts has attracted attention from parties beyond the immediate political establishment."

The way she said it made my royal political training snap to attention. *Parties beyond the immediate political establishment* was diplomatic code for the kind of shadowy factions that operated outside official court structure—groups that had historically responded to threats with elimination rather than negotiation.

"The kind that views your partnership either as a valuable resource to be acquired, or as a threat to be eliminated," Uncle Aldric said with characteristic bluntness. "The magical world is not a peaceful place, Miss Prancer. There are factions that have spent centuries maintaining power through division and conflict. Your ability to create unity threatens their entire foundation."

Through our bond, I felt Fiona's shock as the full scope of what we were facing became clear. We weren't just dealing with academic pressure or court disapproval anymore—we were potentially dealing with people who would kill to prevent the kind of collaborative magic we represented.

Just like they killed Father, I thought, the old grief mixing with new determination. *But this time, we're not facing them alone.*

"We'll protect you," the dean said with the kind of firm authority that suggested the university administration had been preparing for exactly this scenario. "Both of you. The university is implementing enhanced security protocols immediately. Your movements will be monitored, your communications will be secured, and you'll have guards assigned whenever you leave campus."

Guards. I'd lived with security protocols for the first seven years of my life, but Fiona had never experienced the kind of constant surveillance that came with being politically significant. Through our bond, I felt her struggle to process what this would mean for the simple freedoms she'd taken for granted.

"Until we can establish a more permanent solution," Uncle Aldric replied to my question about duration. "Which brings us to the next issue: your future."

With a gesture that I remembered from childhood memories of court sessions, he filled the air with documents that represented the formal legal framework surrounding royal partnerships. Contracts, treaties, agreements written in ancient languages that predated modern magical law.

"Prince Elian, your claiming of Miss Prancer has activated several dormant provisions in inter-court law," he explained, and I felt the weight of centuries of tradition settling over our relationship like a formal cloak. "Most significantly, your partnership must now be formally recognized by all four seasonal courts before it can be considered legally and magically binding."

Four courts. I'd known this moment would come eventually, but seeing it laid out in official documents made the scope of what we were facing undeniably real.

"Trials," Chancellor Arcturus said with obvious displeasure when Fiona asked what formal recognition would involve. "Four separate evaluations, one from each court, testing your compatibility, your magical abilities, and your suitability for the political responsibilities that come with royal partnership."

Through our bond, I felt Fiona's exhaustion at the prospect of more trials. The Frost Trials had been demanding enough, and those had been academic evaluations with university support. What we were facing now would be political theater designed to test not just our magical abilities, but our fitness to influence the future of magical society.

"Much more intensive trials," Magistrate Stormwind corrected when Fiona's tone suggested she thought we were facing more of the same. "The Frost Trials were academic evaluations. What you're facing now are tests that will determine your fitness to help shape the future of our magical society."

But Uncle Aldric's next words carried hope alongside the daunting challenges ahead. "However, there is one advantage to your current situation. The claiming you performed today was witnessed by representatives of multiple courts and recorded by official magical protocols. Rejecting your partnership now would require the courts to publicly admit that their own procedures were flawed."

Political momentum. I recognized the concept from my royal education—the idea that sometimes circumstances aligned to make certain outcomes inevitable regardless of individual preferences.

"You have momentum," Uncle Aldric corrected when I suggested we had leverage. "Use it wisely, because political momentum can disappear as quickly as it appears."

Four months. That's how long we had to prepare for trials that would determine not just our personal future, but potentially the future of collaborative magic itself. It felt like no time at all and an eternity simultaneously.

As the meeting began to wind down and officials prepared to return to their respective duties, I watched Uncle Aldric approach Fiona for a private conversation. Through our bond, I felt her nervousness about speaking privately with someone whose authority she didn't fully understand, but I also sensed his genuine attempt to provide guidance rather than intimidation.

Their conversation was too quiet for me to hear, but I felt Fiona's surprise at his apology, her gratitude for his unexpected praise, and her growing understanding of just how much was at stake in our partnership.

When she rejoined me, I could sense the weight of responsibility settling around her like armor—heavy, but necessary. Protective, even as it limited the casual freedoms she'd enjoyed as a regular student.

"How are you feeling?" I asked as we prepared to leave the conference room, though our bond had already given me glimpses of her emotional state.

"Terrified," she admitted with characteristic honesty. "But also... determined? Is that strange?"

"Not strange at all," I replied, finding her hand with mine as we walked back across campus. "I feel the same way. Like we've finally stopped pretending to be something we're not and started becoming who we were meant to be."

Looking around the campus—at students who now nodded respectfully rather than casually, at the enhanced security measures already being implemented, at the aurora dancing overhead in patterns that seemed to celebrate our claiming—I realized that everything had changed and nothing had changed simultaneously.

We were still partners. We still trusted each other completely. We still created magic together that transcended anything either of us could achieve alone.

But now, instead of hiding that truth, we were stepping into it fully.

"Four months," Fiona said.

"Four months," I agreed. "Think we can master royal diplomatic magic and advanced political theory in four months?"

"With you as my partner?" she smiled, echoing our old refrain with new meaning now that we'd officially committed to facing whatever challenges lay ahead. "I think we can do anything."

The real trials were just beginning, I thought, but looking at Fiona and feeling the absolute certainty of our bond, I believed we were ready for them.

Ready to prove that love and magic could work together to change the world.

Ready to become who we were meant to be—not just as individuals, but as partners who could bridge the artificial divisions that had kept the magical world fragmented for centuries.

CHAPTER TWENTY-THREE
POLITICAL MANEUVERING

FIONA

The first attempt to break our partnership came exactly one week after our public claiming.

I was walking to Advanced Magical Theory when a woman in elegant crimson robes intercepted me outside the Crystal Library. She moved with the fluid grace that marked her as high-level court nobility, and when she smiled, I felt like prey being evaluated by a particularly sophisticated predator.

"Miss Prancer," she said, her voice carrying the kind of cultured accent that spoke of centuries of breeding and education. "How delightful to finally meet you. I am Lady Scorchia, representing certain interests within the Summer Court."

Certain interests. The phrase sent warning bells ringing in my head, but I forced myself to remain polite. "Lady Scorchia. How can I help you?"

"Actually, I was hoping I might help you," she replied, gesturing toward a secluded alcove where we could speak privately. "You see, I've been following your remarkable partnership with Prince Elian with great interest. Quite impressive, really, what you've accomplished."

"Thank you," I said carefully, not moving toward the alcove.

"However," she continued, "I can't help but wonder if you fully understand the position you've placed yourself in. The challenges ahead, the political pressures, the sacrifices that will be required..."

"I understand enough," I replied, though her tone was making me increasingly uncomfortable.

"Do you?" Her smile sharpened. "I know you've been thinking about what it means to become a princess, but have you fully considered the scope of what awaits you? That Prince Elian's eventual queen will need to navigate court intrigue, manage international relations, and make decisions that affect millions of magical beings?"

The word *Queen* hit me like a physical blow. Even though Brynn had mentioned it before, even though I'd been trying not to think about it, hearing it stated so bluntly made the reality impossible to ignore. I'd been focusing on partnership trials and magical bonding, but the ultimate implications of being permanently bound to the heir of a throne were staring me in the face.

"I understand that Elian and I will face those challenges together," I said, lifting my chin despite the uncertainty churning in my stomach.

"Together, yes. But what if there were a way to ensure your partnership could continue without the burden of political responsibility?" Lady Scorchia leaned closer, her voice dropping to a conspiratorial whisper. "What if Prince Elian could abdicate his claim to the throne, freeing you both to pursue your magical collaboration without the weight of royal duty?"

The suggestion was so unexpected that for a moment I

couldn't respond. Elian, giving up his birthright? Abandoning the throne his father had died trying to reform?

"That's not..." I started, then stopped, realizing I didn't actually know what Elian wanted when it came to ruling the Frost Court. We'd been so focused on surviving each immediate crisis that we'd never really discussed long-term plans.

"It's not impossible," Lady Scorchia said, clearly reading my hesitation as interest. "The Summer Court has developed frameworks for magical partnerships that transcend traditional court boundaries. Prince Elian could maintain his royal status while transferring succession rights to a more suitable heir."

"More suitable how?" I asked.

"Someone without the complicated magical entanglements that make traditional court management... challenging." Her smile was razor-sharp. "Someone who could provide the stability that magical society requires while allowing exceptional individuals like yourself and Prince Elian to pursue your collaborative research in peace."

It took me a moment to understand what she was really proposing. "You want Elian to give up his throne so the Summer Court can install someone more favorable to their interests."

"I want Prince Elian to be free to become the magical innovator he's clearly meant to be, rather than being trapped by political obligations he never chose." Her tone was reasonable, sympathetic, and completely persuasive if you ignored the underlying manipulation. "Consider it, Miss Prancer. You could have your partnership without the political pressure. Your magical development without the court intrigue. Your freedom without the sacrifice."

She handed me a small crystal that pulsed with warm golden light. "This contains the complete proposal. Review it at your leisure. I think you'll find it quite generous."

After she left, I stood in the library courtyard for several minutes, turning the crystal over in my hands. The proposal was tempting—more tempting than I wanted to admit. The idea of having our partnership without the crushing weight of royal responsibility, of being able to focus purely on the magical collaboration that had brought us together in the first place...

But something about Lady Scorchia's approach felt wrong. Too convenient, too perfectly tailored to exploit fears I'd barely acknowledged to myself.

I found Elian in his usual morning spot—the Frost Tower observatory, surrounded by charts and documents that looked like they dealt with complex magical theory. When I entered, he looked up with the smile that never failed to make my heart skip a beat.

"How was Advanced Theory?" he asked, then paused when he saw my expression. "What's wrong?"

I told him about Lady Scorchia's visit, about the proposal for abdication, about the offer to free us from political responsibility. As I spoke, I watched his expression grow increasingly troubled.

"She approached you directly?" he asked when I finished. "Without going through official channels or requesting permission from university administration?"

"Is that significant?"

"It means this isn't an official Summer Court proposal—it's a private initiative by someone with their own agenda." He stood and began pacing, his movement sharp with barely contained anger. "And it means they're trying to manipulate you into influencing my decisions rather than dealing with me directly."

"Why would they do that?"

"Because they think you're the weak link in our partnership. That you'll crack under pressure and convince me to abandon my responsibilities rather than face them together." His pale eyes blazed with fury. "They're betting that your feelings for me will make you prioritize our personal happiness over political duty."

The words stung because they contained a grain of truth. Part of me had been tempted by Lady Scorchia's offer, had imagined how much simpler our lives could be without the weight of royal expectations.

"Were they right?" Elian asked quietly, and I could hear the vulnerability underneath his anger.

"No," I said, surprising myself with the firmness of my response. "They weren't right. Because giving up your birthright wouldn't solve anything—it would just prove that collaborative magic partnerships can't handle real responsibility."

I moved to stand in front of him, close enough that I could see the flecks of silver in his ice-blue eyes. "Elian, your father died believing that magical collaboration could change society for the better. Running away from the throne because it's difficult would dishonor everything he sacrificed."

"Even if it means years of political pressure, diplomatic trials, and constant scrutiny of our every decision?"

"Even then." I reached for his hands, feeling our bond flare with shared determination. "We're not just building a partnership anymore—we're proving that love and magic can work together to create something better than what came before. That's not something we can do from the sidelines."

Relief flooded through our connection, and I realized that Elian had been testing me as much as asking for reassurance. He needed to know that I was committed to the full scope of what we were building, not just the easy parts.

"There's something else," I said, pulling the crystal from my pocket. "Lady Scorchia gave me this. She said it contains the complete proposal."

Elian studied the crystal with obvious distaste. "We should

examine it together. If we're going to reject their offer, we need to understand exactly what we're rejecting."

We spent the next hour analyzing the contents of the crystal, and what we found was both impressive and deeply troubling. The Summer Court's proposal was indeed generous—they offered to facilitate Elian's abdication in exchange for installing his cousin Marcus as the new Frost Court heir, while providing us with protected status as "magical researchers" under Summer Court patronage.

But the fine print revealed the true cost: we would be essentially purchased by the Summer Court, our magical development guided by their priorities rather than our own choices. Our partnership would continue, but only as long as it served their political interests.

"It's a gilded cage," Elian said with disgust. "They want to neutralize the threat we represent by making us their pet project rather than independent agents of change."

"And if we refuse?"

"Then they'll try other approaches. Political pressure, economic sanctions against the Frost Court, attempts to undermine our partnership through more direct means." He was quiet for a moment, studying the crystal's contents. "This is just the beginning, Fiona. Every court has its own agenda, its own vision for how to handle what we represent."

As if summoned by his words, Professor Blitzen's voice echoed through the observatory via magical communication spell.

"Prince Elian, Miss Prancer, please report to my office immediately. We have a situation."

We found Professor Blitzen's office crowded with people I was beginning to recognize as the key players in our unfolding political drama. Lord Frostborn sat behind the desk, his expression grimmer than usual. Chancellor Arcturus occupied a chair near the window, while Magistrate Stormwind appeared via magical projection. But it was the new figure that caught my attention—a man in deep green robes whose very presence made the plants in the office grow visibly larger.

"Prince Elian, Miss Prancer," Lord Frostborn said without preamble, "may I present Lord Thornfield, representing the Spring Court's interests in your partnership."

"Your Highness, Miss Prancer," Lord Thornfield said, inclining his head formally. "I bring greetings from the Spring Court and an invitation to discuss your future."

Another invitation. I exchanged glances with Elian, seeing my own wariness reflected in his expression.

"What kind of discussion?" Elian asked.

"The kind that recognizes the unprecedented nature of your partnership and seeks to provide appropriate support for its development," Lord Thornfield replied smoothly. "The Spring Court has always valued innovation and growth. Your collaborative magic represents exactly the kind of evolution we've been hoping to see in inter-court relations."

"Unlike the Summer Court's approach," Chancellor Arcturus observed acidly, "which seems to involve acquiring promising partnerships rather than supporting them."

"You know about Lady Scorchia's visit?" I asked.

"Word travels quickly in magical political circles," Magistrate Stormwind said with obvious disapproval. "The Summer Court's attempt to recruit you through private channels rather than official diplomatic procedures has caused considerable concern among the other courts."

"Because it suggests they view your partnership as a resource to be acquired rather than a development to be supported," Lord Thornfield added. "The Spring Court, by contrast, believes that magical partnerships of your caliber should be nurtured in their natural environment rather than transplanted for political convenience."

The difference in approach was subtle but significant. Where the Summer Court wanted to own us, the Spring Court seemed to want to sponsor us. Still problematic, but less immediately threatening.

"What exactly are you proposing?" Elian asked.

"Enhanced training opportunities, access to Spring Court magical archives, and protection from political pressure during your development period," Lord Thornfield replied. "In exchange, we would ask only for the opportunity to study your collaborative techniques and occasional consultation on inter-court magical policy."

"And the catch?" I asked, because there was always a catch.

"No catch, per se. But your partnership would become a showcase for Spring Court values—growth, innovation, and collaboration. You would be expected to represent those values in your public appearances and political statements."

Another gilded cage, just painted a different color.

"I think," Elian said carefully, "that we need time to consider our options. This is all happening very quickly."

"Of course," Lord Thornfield said graciously. "Though I should mention that the Autumn Court has also expressed interest in meeting with you. And I believe the Winter Court will want to present their own proposal soon."

All four courts. Every major magical authority wanted to claim some influence over our partnership, to shape our development according to their own agenda.

"Wonderful," I muttered.

After the various officials left, Elian and I sat alone in Professor Blitzen's office, the weight of political maneuvering settling around us like fog.

"Four different courts, four different agendas," Elian said wearily. "And all of them convinced they know what's best for our partnership."

"What do we do?" I asked.

"We remember that this is exactly what my father faced—political pressure to conform, to compromise, to let other people's fears limit what collaborative magic could become." Elian's voice grew stronger, more determined. "And we choose the same path he did. We stay true to our vision, regardless of who tries to buy us, control us, or manipulate us."

"Even if it means making enemies of people who could have been allies?"

"Especially then," he replied. "Because the moment we start making decisions based on political convenience rather than magical truth, we become just another court asset instead of agents of real change."

Looking at him—seeing the strength and conviction that had been forged through twenty years of hiding and testing—I felt a surge of fierce pride. This was why I'd claimed him. Not because he was a prince, but because he was someone who would choose the difficult right path over the easy wrong one.

"Together?" I asked, echoing our first conversation about trust.

"Always," he replied.

But as we prepared to face the remaining court delegations and their competing agendas, I realized that the magical trials had been the easy part.

The real test would be staying true to ourselves while the entire magical world tried to reshape us according to their own vision of what we should become.

The question was whether our love and partnership would be

strong enough to resist forces that had been shaping magical society for centuries.

Looking at Elian, feeling the absolute certainty of our bond, I thought they would be.

But I was also beginning to understand that believing it and proving it were two entirely different things.

CHAPTER TWENTY-FOUR
WINTER BALL

ELIAN

The announcement came three weeks after the court delegations had finished their recruitment attempts, arriving via enchanted courier with the kind of formal pomp that immediately activated my political survival instincts. North Pole University would host its annual Winter Ball, and this year's celebration would formally recognize the new political realities that our partnership had created.

A final examination, I thought, studying the invitation's crystalline lettering that shifted between silver and gold, sealed with the combined crests of all four seasonal courts. *They want to see how we handle ourselves under the most public scrutiny possible.*

"It's a trap," Brynn said bluntly as our small strategy session gathered in Fiona's dormitory room. The space felt cramped with most of our original network present, but I appreciated their willingness to stand with us despite the political pressure that association with us now carried.

"Of course it's a trap," Fiona agreed, and through our bond, I felt her mixture of resignation and determination. "The question is whether it's a trap we can survive."

"Or turn to our advantage," I added, moving to the window where I could observe the preparations taking place across campus. Workers hung lights that captured and reflected aurora patterns with precision that suggested court-level magical artisans. Gardeners coaxed winter roses to bloom in impossible arrangements that would have been considered minor miracles in less magical circumstances. Even the catering staff was testing dishes that sparkled with edible magic sophisticated enough to impress the most discerning court palates.

They're not taking any chances with the presentation, I observed. *This ball will be a showcase of NPU's capabilities, designed to demonstrate that the university can host events worthy of inter-court political importance.*

"How is a formal ball where we'll be surrounded by representatives from every major court in the realm possibly to our advantage?" Marcus asked, his practical mind cutting straight to the tactical concerns.

"Because it's public," I replied, my royal political training helping me see the strategic opportunities. "All the political maneuvering of the past few weeks has happened in private meetings, closed-door negotiations, and subtle pressure applied away from public scrutiny. But a formal ball... that's theater. Performance. Everyone will be watching to see how we handle ourselves."

Through our bond, I felt Fiona's understanding click into place. She was beginning to see what I'd learned during my years in hiding: sometimes the most dangerous situations were also the most liberating, because public scrutiny constrained everyone's behavior, not just ours.

"But if we handle ourselves well?" Brynn prompted.

"Then we prove that love and magic can create something stronger than political manipulation," I said, leaving my position by the window to join their huddle. "We show everyone that collaborative partnerships don't have to choose between personal happiness and political responsibility."

The weight of that expectation settled over the room, and through our bond, I felt Fiona's recognition of just how much was riding on a single evening's performance. This wasn't just about surviving a formal dinner and some dancing. This was about demonstrating our fitness to help reshape the future of magical society.

"So what's our strategy?" Marcus asked.

I looked at Fiona, seeing my own determination reflected in her green eyes. "We be ourselves. Completely, authentically, without apology or compromise. We show them exactly what our partnership looks like when it's operating at full strength."

"That's it?" Brynn asked skeptically. "That's the plan?"

"That's the plan," I confirmed, drawing on lessons learned through twenty years of careful survival. "Because the moment we start performing for their expectations instead of being true to our own values, we lose everything that makes our partnership worth preserving."

Two days later, I stood in my observatory chambers, adjusting the ceremonial collar of formal court robes I hadn't worn since I was seven years old. The silver-white fabric carried frost patterns embroidered in threads that seemed to capture and reflect light, cut with the unmistakable lines that marked formal Frost Court regalia. But it was more than clothing—it was a declaration of identity, a public acceptance of the royal heritage I'd spent two decades hiding.

Prince Elian Frostborn, I thought, studying my reflection in the crystalline mirror. *Not the anonymous transfer student, not the hidden heir, but exactly who I was born to be.*

The knock on my door came precisely when I expected it. Through our bond, I could feel Fiona's mixture of nervousness and anticipation, her own transformation into someone ready to stand beside royalty at the most formal political event either of us had ever attended.

When I opened the door, the sight of her made my breath catch completely.

She wore midnight blue silk that seemed to capture starlight in its folds, with silver threading that traced patterns reminiscent of frost and aurora light. The dress had been a gift from Lady Silverwind—a political gesture as much as personal kindness, marking the Enclave's continued support for our partnership. But it was perfect for Fiona, formal enough for a royal function while remaining recognizably her.

She looks like a princess, I thought, and felt her startled reaction through our bond as she caught the edge of that thought.

"You're beautiful," I said simply, letting her see in my expression exactly how magnificent I found her—not just physically, but as a partner who was stepping into political responsibility with grace and courage.

"So are you," she replied, moving to straighten my ceremonial collar, though it didn't need adjustment. The simple touch sent warmth through our bond that steadied both of us. "Ready for this?"

"With you as my partner?" I smiled, our old refrain carrying new weight now that we were about to face the most public test of our relationship. "I think we can handle anything."

The Grand Ballroom had been transformed into something that would have impressed even the most demanding court officials from my childhood memories. Crystal chandeliers cast rainbow patterns across walls that seemed made of compressed starlight, while the ceiling showed a perfect view of the aurora borealis. The floor reflected the lights above like a mirror made of polished winter sky, and everywhere I looked, winter roses bloomed in impossible shades of silver and gold.

But it was the guests that activated every piece of political training I'd ever received.

Representatives from all four seasonal courts filled the ballroom in a formal arrangement that spoke of careful diplomatic protocol. I spotted Uncle Aldric near the Frost Court delegation, his expression carefully neutral as he surveyed the crowd with the same analytical attention I was applying to the political landscape. Lady Scorchia held court near the Summer Court's table, her crimson dress making her look like a living flame among the cooler colors surrounding her. Lord Thornfield moved through the crowd with practiced diplomatic grace, while Autumn Court representatives created their own cluster of burgundy and gold that spoke of harvest abundance and political prosperity.

And above it all, in a section that seemed to float independently of the rest of the ballroom, sat the Council of Seasonal Balance—the three most powerful magical authorities in the realm, here to witness whatever political theater tonight would bring.

The entire magical establishment, I realized, *gathered to evaluate whether we're worth the disruption we've caused to their carefully maintained status quo.*

"Breathe," I murmured to Fiona as we paused at the entrance for the formal announcements, though I was giving myself the same advice.

"Prince Elian Frostborn," the herald called, his voice carrying easily through the vast space, "heir to the Frost Court, and his chosen partner, Miss Fiona Prancer of the Prancer reindeer shifting clan."

The ballroom fell silent as we began our formal entrance, and I felt the weight of hundreds of eyes studying our every movement with laser intensity. But instead of the intimidation I might have expected, I felt something closer to pride.

Look at us, I thought, taking in our reflection in the polished floor as we walked. *We belong together in a way that's visible to everyone watching.*

Our magic naturally harmonized as we moved, creating subtle light displays that spoke of partnership rather than individual power. We unconsciously matched each other's pace and bearing, moving together with the kind of synchronization that couldn't be faked or taught. Most importantly, we both carried ourselves with quiet confidence despite the obvious political pressure, proving that our bond had made us stronger rather than more vulnerable.

"They're beautiful together," I heard someone whisper, and felt Fiona's flush of pleasure through our bond.

"Powerful," another voice added with what sounded like genuine admiration. "Look at the magical resonance they're generating without even trying."

We were seated at the high table, positioned between Uncle Aldric and Professor Blitzen—a placement that clearly indicated our elevated status while keeping us surrounded by allies. The symbolic importance wasn't lost on me; they were treating us as honored guests rather than students under evaluation.

The dinner that followed was a masterwork of diplomatic cuisine, each course designed to showcase collaborative potential between different magical traditions. Spring Court vegetables that grew as you watched them, Summer Court fruits that tasted like concentrated sunshine, Autumn Court grains that carried the essence of successful harvests, and Winter Court ice wines that somehow managed to be both refreshing and warming.

"A diplomatic menu," I observed quietly to Fiona, recognizing the political messaging in every dish. "Showing that collaboration between courts can create something better than any individual contribution."

"Think that's intentional?" she asked.

"Absolutely. Everything tonight is symbolic."

And it was. The seating arrangements spoke of political alliances, the menu choices demonstrated collaborative potential, and even the music was carefully selected to represent all four seasonal traditions in harmony. At the center of it all, we were being evaluated not just for our magical abilities but for our understanding of the political theater we were participating in.

As the formal dinner concluded and the dancing began, I felt our real test approaching. This would be the most public display of our partnership, where every gesture would be analyzed and every magical manifestation would be studied for political implications.

"May I have this dance?" I asked formally, offering my hand with the courtly grace that reminded everyone watching of my royal heritage.

"Always," she replied, accepting my hand and letting me lead her onto the dance floor.

The moment we began to move together, our magic responded with controlled beauty that surpassed anything we'd achieved in private practice. Golden and silver light spiraled around us, but this wasn't the chaotic overflow we'd sometimes experienced during training. This was purposeful artistry, controlled power, the visible manifestation of a partnership that had been tested and proven unbreakable.

We're telling a story, I realized as we moved through the

complex patterns of formal court dancing. *Not just with our move-*
ments, but with our magic—the story of two people from different
worlds who found something worth fighting for together.

Other couples joined us on the dance floor, but we remained
the center of attention. Through my peripheral vision, I could see
court representatives leaning forward to better observe our
magical displays, professors taking notes on collaborative techniques we were demonstrating unconsciously, even Council
members watching with expressions that mixed approval with
concern about implications they were still calculating.

"They're seeing it," I said quietly to Fiona as we moved
through a complex turn that sent spirals of light cascading around
us. "What we really are when we're working together."

"Good or bad?" she asked.

"Both, probably. But honest."

As the dance concluded and we returned to our seats, I felt the
deep satisfaction of a performance that had revealed truth rather
than concealing it. We had shown them exactly what our partnership looked like at its best—powerful, harmonious, and utterly
committed to something larger than individual ambition.

But the evening's real test came during the formal presenta-
tions, when political positions would be declared publicly rather
than negotiated in private.

"Prince Elian," Uncle Aldric announced, rising from his seat
with the ceremonial dignity that marked formal court pronounce-
ments. "As heir to the Frost Court and representative of ancient
collaborative traditions, you have demonstrated exceptional
magical ability and political maturity. The Frost Court formally
recognizes your partnership with Miss Fiona Prancer and
commits to supporting your continued development."

The applause that filled the ballroom carried political weight
beyond mere congratulation. This was a public declaration of alle-

giance that would affect inter-court relations for years to come, Uncle Aldric's way of ensuring that opposing our partnership would require opposing the Frost Court itself.

"Furthermore," he continued, "the Frost Court announces the establishment of the Prancer-Frost Collaborative Magic Research Initiative, designed to study and develop the techniques you have pioneered."

Brilliant, I thought as more applause rose with undercurrents of surprise and speculation. By creating an official framework around our partnership, he was giving it institutional support that would be much harder for opposing factions to dismantle through political maneuvering.

"The Spring Court joins the Frost Court in recognizing this partnership," Lord Thornfield said, rising in response, "and pledges our resources to support collaborative magic research that benefits all courts."

"As does the Summer Court," Lady Scorchia added, though her tone suggested this wasn't her preferred outcome. Political momentum had reached the point where opposition was no longer viable, forcing even reluctant courts to offer public support.

One by one, representatives from every major court offered their formal recognition. Not because they all believed in what we were doing, but because the political cost of opposition had become too high to sustain.

"Miss Prancer," Magistrate Stormwind said, her voice carrying from the floating Council platform, "you have demonstrated exceptional grace under pressure and wisdom beyond your years. The Council of Seasonal Balance formally recognizes your partnership with Prince Elian and commits to ensuring that collaborative magic development receives the support and oversight necessary for success."

As the formal recognitions concluded and the evening began to wind down, I felt something I hadn't experienced since childhood: complete political victory achieved through authenticity rather than manipulation.

"How do you feel?" I asked Fiona as we prepared to leave.

"Like we just won a war without having to fight a battle," she replied, and through our bond, I felt her matching sense of triumph. "Like we proved that being authentic and committed was stronger than any political maneuvering they could attempt."

"The real work starts now," I said, though I was smiling with the satisfaction of someone who had just proven that his father's vision was not only possible but inevitable. "Building the research initiative, working with the courts, proving that what we've started can benefit everyone rather than threatening established power structures."

As the Winter Ball concluded and guests began to depart, many stopped to offer personal congratulations and express interest in our future work. The young Spring Court representative who had been affected by our magical network during the trials approached with obvious nervousness but genuine enthusiasm.

"Your Highness, Miss Prancer," he said formally, "I wanted to thank you for what you shared with us during the trials. The experience of genuine collaborative magic... it's changed how I think about everything."

"That's exactly what we hoped for," Fiona replied warmly. "Change starts with individual understanding, then grows into collective transformation."

"We'll be accepting anyone who's committed to learning and growing," I added when he asked about the research initiative. "Collaboration works best when it includes diverse perspectives and fresh ideas."

The next generation, I thought, watching his face light up with hope. *They'll have opportunities my father could never have imagined.*

As we finally made our way across campus, the winter air crisp with promise and the aurora dancing overhead in celebration, I felt a profound sense of completion mixed with anticipation.

We had done more than survive the political pressure—we had transformed it into momentum for change. We had proven our partnership could not only handle scrutiny but could inspire others to believe in collaborative magic.

"Thank you," Fiona said as we paused outside Shifter Lodge.

"For what?"

"For choosing me. For trusting me with your real identity, your political future, your magical destiny," she said, reaching for my hands. "For proving that love and magic can work together to create something extraordinary."

"Thank you," I replied, "for seeing who I could become when I was still afraid to see it myself. For choosing to fight for this partnership when it would have been safer to walk away. For showing me that collaboration isn't weakness—it's the strongest magic of all."

When I kissed her, the aurora above us flared brighter, and I could have sworn I heard the distant sound of bells ringing in celebration—not just of our personal happiness, but of the transformation we represented for magical society itself.

Tomorrow would bring new challenges as we built the research initiative, worked with court representatives, and proved that collaborative magic could benefit everyone rather than threatening established power structures. But tonight, surrounded by evidence of how far we'd come and promises of where we could go, I felt nothing but hope.

We were exactly what we'd been meant to become from the

moment our names had appeared together on that crystal board: partners, equals, and the beginning of something that could transform magical society for the better.

Looking at Fiona, feeling the absolute certainty of our bond and the support of institutions that had recognized our value, I knew we were ready for whatever came next.

After all, we'd already proven that dangerous things could also be beautiful.

EPILOGUE: THE FOUR COURTS TRIALS

FOUR MONTHS LATER - END OF SPRING TERM

The Grand Amphitheater of the Four Courts had been carved from a single massive glacier that somehow managed to be both ancient and eternal. Representatives from Winter, Spring, Summer, and Autumn occupied crystalline viewing boxes that floated at different heights around the central arena, their formal robes creating a rainbow of seasonal authority.

I stood in the center of the arena with Elian, our hands linked not just for moral support but because our magic had grown so intertwined over the months that separation felt physically uncomfortable. The audience included not just court officials, but university faculty, family members, and what seemed like half the magical world's political establishment.

No pressure whatsoever.

"The trials will consist of three phases," announced Magistrate Stormwind, her voice carrying easily through the vast space despite speaking without magical amplification. "Individual demonstration, collaborative creation, and crisis response. All four courts will evaluate each according to criteria of technical skill, innovative application, political wisdom, and partnership stability."

Beside me, Elian's ice-blue eyes held steady confidence despite the magnitude of what we were facing. The past few months had tested us in ways I'd never imagined—not just magically, but politically, emotionally, and personally. Court officials had observed every one of our training sessions. Political pressure had mounted from factions who saw our partnership as either a valuable asset or an existential threat.

But we'd survived it all. More than survived—we'd grown stronger.

"Miss Prancer," Magistrate Stormwind called. "You will go first."

I stepped forward onto the raised platform, acutely aware of hundreds of eyes studying my every movement.

No pressure.

I closed my eyes and reached for my magic, but instead of the familiar golden warmth, I found something deeper. The intensive training of the past months had changed me, connected me to power that felt both ancient and absolutely right.

When I opened my eyes, light was spiraling around me in patterns that told the story of everything we'd discovered together. Not just magical techniques, but the deeper truth that individual strength multiplied exponentially when shared with the right partner.

Golden light wove through the air above the arena, showing visions of what collaborative magic could accomplish. Partnerships that bridged species barriers, magic that healed instead of harmed, a future where cooperation replaced competition as the driving force of magical society.

When the magic finally settled, the amphitheater was silent

except for the soft sound of someone weeping in the Autumn Court section. Then, slowly, applause began—not the polite acknowledgment I'd expected, but genuine appreciation for something that had moved them.

"Prince Elian," Magistrate Stormwind called.

Elian stepped forward, and immediately the temperature in the arena dropped. But this wasn't just a demonstration of raw power—it was artistry, precision, and hope given crystalline form.

Ice erupted from the platform in spiraling towers that caught and reflected the aurora light dancing overhead. But woven through every structure were patterns that matched the rhythm of my magical signature, proving that even in individual performance, he understood that true strength came through connection rather than isolation.

By the time he finished, the arena had been transformed into a winter cathedral so beautiful that several audience members were openly staring in wonder.

"Phase Two," Magistrate Stormwind announced. "Collaborative creation."

This was what we'd been training for—the chance to show what we could accomplish when our magic flowed together without reservation or fear.

I moved to Elian's side, and the moment our hands touched, golden warmth met crystalline precision in perfect harmony. What we built together defied every rule of magical theory I'd ever learned.

Light and ice wove together into something that seemed alive, responding not just to our conscious direction but to the deeper truths that flowed through our bond. The construct grew and evolved, showing scenes of magical partnerships that could reshape society, techniques that required multiple types of power to achieve their full potential, and a vision of what the world could become if artificial barriers were dissolved in favor of genuine collaboration.

By the time we finished, the entire arena was filled with light and ice in perfect balance, creating an environment so harmonious that the very air seemed to sing.

The applause this time was thunderous, but I barely heard it. I was lost in the afterglow of our magic, in the absolute rightness of what we'd created together.

"Phase Three," Magistrate Stormwind announced, and her tone carried new gravity. "Crisis response."

The beautiful structure we'd created dissolved, replaced by something that made my blood run cold. The arena floor opened to reveal a simulation of magical disaster—chaotic energy that threatened to consume everything in its path, civilian constructs trapped in the center of the maelstrom.

"Much like the last trail, a magical catastrophe has occurred during a diplomatic gathering," the magistrate explained. "Rescue the civilians, contain the chaotic energy, and prevent the disaster from spreading beyond this arena. Failure will result in immediate disqualification."

Immediate disqualification. After everything we'd been through, everything we'd proved, it could all end here if we couldn't rise to this final challenge.

"Ready?" Elian asked, ice already beginning to spiral around his hands.

"Ready," I replied, golden fire dancing around my fingers.

What followed was the most intense magical collaboration of my life. The chaotic energy fought against our attempts to contain it, actively trying to disrupt our partnership and force us apart. But every month of training, every challenge we'd faced, every moment of trust we'd built came together in perfect synchronization.

Where I provided flexibility and adaptability, Elian anchored our efforts with precision and structure. Where his royal training gave us strategic thinking, my shifter instincts guided us toward solutions that pure logic couldn't reach. We weren't just two people working together—we were a single magical entity with twice the capability of either individual.

By the time we'd rescued the last civilian construct and sealed the chaotic energy into stable containment, the arena had once again been transformed. This time, instead of art, we'd created something more precious: proof that collaborative magic could handle any crisis, solve any problem, protect anyone who needed protection.

As the arena returned to normal and the monitoring equipment powered down, I felt a deep sense of completion. Whatever the courts decided, we had proven beyond any doubt that our partnership was not just viable, but revolutionary.

"The trials are concluded," Magistrate Stormwind announced. "The evaluation committee will now deliberate."

An hour later, we stood before representatives of all four courts to hear our fate.

"Miss Prancer, Prince Elian," Magistrate Stormwind began, "the highest magical authorities have evaluated your performance today in the realm. The committee's decision is unanimous."

My heart hammered against my ribs as I waited for words that would either validate everything we'd built or destroy it entirely.

"Your partnership has demonstrated not only exceptional magical capability, but the potential to advance collaborative magic theory by decades. The Four Courts formally recognize your bond and commit to supporting its continued development."

Relief flooded through me so intensely that I nearly collapsed. We'd done it. We'd proven that love and magic could work together to create something extraordinary.

"Furthermore," she continued, "you are hereby granted special dispensation to establish the first Inter-Court Collaborative Magic Research Program, to be housed at North Pole University under joint oversight from all seasonal courts."

A research program. Our own research program, where we could explore collaborative magic theory without political interference or academic limitations.

"However," she added, and my relief crystallized into caution, "this recognition comes with significant responsibility. Your partnership will be closely monitored, your research will have political implications, and your choices will affect magical society for generations to come."

"We understand," Elian said, his voice carrying the authority he'd been born to wield. "And we accept that responsibility."

Looking at the representatives of all four courts, seeing approval where there had once been suspicion, I felt something settle in my chest that I'd never experienced before: certainty. Not just about our partnership, but about our purpose.

We weren't just students anymore. We weren't just a couple navigating the complications of magical politics. We were pioneers, proving that collaborative magic could create a better future for everyone.

As we left the amphitheater hand in hand, magical energy still humming between us in perfect harmony, I caught sight of Connor and Kayla in the audience. Connor gave me a thumbs up and a grin that said he'd known all along we'd succeed. Kayla blew me a kiss and mouthed, "So proud of you."

We walked across the campus of North Pole University as the northern lights danced overhead in celebration. I was simply

Fiona Prancer, magical researcher, royal partner, and the happiest person in the magical world.

"So," Elian said as we reached the steps of Shifter Lodge, where Brynn and Marcus were waiting with champagne and congratulations, "think you're ready for whatever comes next?"

I looked at him—seeing not a hidden prince or a political complication, but simply the person I'd chosen to love and build a future with. The person who'd proven that some partnerships were worth any risk to preserve.

"With you as my partner?" I smiled, our old call-and-response taking on new meaning now that we'd officially conquered the magical world together. "I think we can change everything."

"Good," he replied, pulling me closer as our friends surrounded us with celebration and our magic painted aurora patterns across the evening sky. "Because changing everything is exactly what we're going to do."

The trials were over. Our real work was just beginning.

And I couldn't wait to get started.

The End.

Did you enjoy *Freshman Frost*?

Please consider leaving a review on Goodreads, Bookbub or your favorite retailer. Reviews help me reach new readers.

Read **Sophomore Solstice** the next book in the **North Pole University** series.

Join my Newsletter for weekly writing updates, exclusive content, new releases, sales, and promotions.

ABOUT THE AUTHOR

Positive, uplifting books and stories.

Marie-Hélène Lebeault is the author of *The Evers Series, Clarity Castle, What Happens Next? Readers Decide Which Story Becomes a Book, the Blood Magick Trilogy, Holiday Shifters, Ghost Stories, Defenders of the Realm, Utopia, Chronicles of the Starborne Cadets, Legends Reborn*, as well as a series of picture books called Fairy Grandmother. She lives in Canada with her grown children.

www.mhlebeault.com

Follow on Social Media, she'd love to hear from you!

f facebook.com/mhlebeaultauthor

X x.com/mhlebeault

O instagram.com/mhlebeault

a amazon.com/author/mhlebeault

BB bookbub.com/authors/marie-helene-lebeault

g goodreads.com/mhlebeault

in linkedin.com/in/mhlebeault

d tiktok.com/@mhlebeaultauthor

ALSO BY THE AUTHOR

North Pole University - NA Paranormal Romance

Holiday Shifters

Freshman Frost

Sophomore Solstice

Junior Jinx

Senior Spark

Wedded Bliss

Mistletoe Misfits

Legends Reborn - NA Fairytale Retellings

A Curse of Snow and Ash

A Curse of Thorns and Slumber

A Curse of Glass and Shadows

A Curse of Scars and Silver

The Chronicles of the Starborne Cadets - YA Space Opera

Confluence of Destinies (Prequel)

Stars Beyond Realms

Shadows of Orion

Echoes of the Void

The Nebula's Heart

The Starborne Paradox

Defenders of the Realm - YA Epic Fantasy

A Journey to Power

The Quest for the Emerald Rattleback

A Summer of Discovery

The Quest for the Sacred Tree

A Summer of Opposites

The Quest for the Phantom Feather

A Summer of Courage

The Quest for the Kraken's Ink

A Summer of Destiny

The Quest for the Cursed Mirrors

A Summer of Unity

Defenders of the Realm - Special Edition Hardcover Set

The Evers Series - YA Science Fantasy

The Ancestors' Key

The Academy

The Time Walker

The World Jumper

5th Anniversary Edition Omnibus

The Traveler's Handbook

The Lost Key

Blood Magick Trilogy - YA Urban Fantasy

The Blood Mage

Blood Magick

Blood Legacy

Extended Edition Omnibus

Standalones

Clarity Castle

What Happens Next?

Ghost Stories

Echoes of Tomorrow

Utopia

Picture Books

Fairy Grandmother: Millie Goes to Antarctica

Fairy Grandmother: Millie Goes to the North Pole

Fairy Grandmother: Millie Goes to China

Fairy Grandmother: Millie Goes to Africa

(Also available in French, Spanish, German, and Italian)